HAUNTED HARBOURS

HAUNTED HARBOURS

Ghost Stories
from old Nova Scotia

Steve Vernon

NIMBUS
PUBLISHING

Nimbus Publishing Limited
PO Box 9166
Halifax, NS B3K 5M8
(902) 455-4286

Printed and bound in Canada

Cover Design: Michael Little, Ideas Ink Design
Interior Design: John van der Woude

Library and Archives Canada Cataloguing in Publication

Vernon, Steve
Haunted harbours : ghost stories from
old Nova Scotia / Steve Vernon.

ISBN 1-55109-592-0
1. Ghosts–Nova Scotia. 2. Folklore–Nova Scotia. I. Title.
BF1472.C3V47 2006   398.209716'05   C2006-904151-2

Canadä   The Canada Council | Le Conseil des Arts
for the Arts | du Canada

We acknowledge the financial support of the Government of Canada through the Book Publishing Industry Development Program (BPIDP) and the Canada Council, and of the Province of Nova Scotia through the Department of Tourism, Culture and Heritage for our publishing activities.

The past is a ghost,
the future is a dream,
and all that's precious
lies in between.

N

Cape North

Sydney

Northumberland Strait

Antigonish Harbour

Antigonish

Isaac's Harbour

Sable Island

Five Islands
Parrsboro

Wittenburg

Mushaboom

Morden

Windsor

Halifax

Devil's Island

Mahone Bay
Lunenburg

Atlantic Ocean

Liverpool

Jordan Falls

Yarmouth

Mud Island

The past is a ghost,
the future is a dream,
and all that's precious
lies in between.

Cape North

Sydney

Northumberland Strait

Antigonish
Harbour

Antigonish

Isaac's Harbour

Sable Island

Five Islands
Parrsboro

Wittenburg

Mushaboom

Morden

Windsor

Halifax

Devil's Island

Mahone Bay
Lunenburg

Atlantic Ocean

Liverpool

Jordan Falls

Yarmouth

Mud Island

CONTENTS

Introduction   1

1 The Piecemeal Ghost of Black Rock Beach (Halifax)   6

2 The Restless Spirits of Devil's Island (Devil's Island)   14

3 The Tale of the *Young Teazer* (Mahone Bay)   18

4 Old Nick Is Ringing His Bell (Lunenburg)   23

5 The Ghost-Hunter's Whistling Ghost (Liverpool)   30

6 The Jordan Falls Forerunner (Jordan Falls)   35

7 As Pale As Ice and As Hard As Stone (Mud Island)   40

8 The Captain's House at Yarmouth (Yarmouth)   45

9 The Iron Box at French Cross (Morden)   49

10 The Piper's Pond Pibroch (Windsor)   54

11 The Moose Island Devil (Five Islands)   60

12 The Weeping Cave of Parrsboro (Parrsboro)   66

13 The Hidey Hinder of Dagger Woods (Antigonish)   70

14 The Black Dog of Antigonish Harbour (Antigonish Harbour)   77

15 The Cape North Selkie (Cape North)   82

16 The Song of the Pit Pony (Sydney)   88

17 Blood in the Water, Blood on the Sand (Sable Island)   93

18 The Phantom Oarsman of Sable Island (Sable Island)   97

19 The Salt Man of Isaac's Harbour (Isaac's Harbour)   103

20 Big Tony and the Moose (Mushaboom)   107

21 The Yonderstone of Wittenburg Cemetery (Wittenburg)   113

Last Words   118

INTRODUCTION

It was an early October morning and the wind was gossiping with the trees of University Avenue. I could hear Old Man Winter chuckling softly just around the corner of the year, rubbing his icy blue palms together, just tickled at the thought of the great cold and white practical joke he was getting ready to play.

Halifax was just waking up. All across the city people were getting out of bed and sliding slices of Ben's bread into the mouths of their toasters, frying eggs and pouring cereal and perking good black coffee. The Bedford Highway was already jam-packed with weary motorized pilgrims making their way in. The bridges were equally crowded. Everybody was heading towards work, and I was no exception. I walked into the

1

Public Archives, marched up to the desk, and smiled charmingly at the young woman who sat behind it. There was a man at the bank of computers by the windows, using the Internet. His hair was tinted so many colours that it looked like he'd washed it in a box of crayons. He had so many facial piercings that I wondered if he'd recently fallen face-first into a fistful of fishing tackle.

"Do you have your card?" asked the woman at the desk.

I handed her my Archives identity card, trying very hard not to think of a hundred old war movies with the secret police in menacing trench coats hissing, "Papers, please."

This wasn't the first time I'd been here. I'd been researching this collection for more than a year, gathering stories from hearsay and recollection, notes, diaries, and history books. I was used to the security the Archives demanded. They have every right to be careful; there is a lot of irreplaceable information stored inside these heavy stone walls. The Archives has been gathering it since 1929, when Premier Rhodes first laid the cornerstone of the original Studley Campus Archives, with a solid silver masonry trowel. Back then, the Archives were housed in a small stone structure close to the Dalhousie Arts and Administration Building. It was the gift of an anonymous donor who was later "outed" as William H. Chase, the Apple King of Nova Scotia, a good man right down to the core.

In 1980 the old Archives was moved to its current location at 6016 University Avenue, and the old building was turned over to the Mathematics Department of Dalhousie University, which still occupies it.

Which brings me right back to the beginning of my story, which is the proper place to start. I'm a storyteller, born in the woods of the North Canadian Shield. I learned the storytelling tradition from my grandfather. Since he was too old for tag or hide-and-seek, he'd tell me stories and get me to tell them back to him. Nowadays I make a bit of a living working through the Nova Scotia Writers' Federation's Writers in the Schools program. I visit schools across the Maritimes, talking to kids from the early grades right on up to high school, teaching them how to tell and write stories.

On this day, I was at the Archives, putting together a collection of Maritime ghost stories. I was a man on a mission, a man with a plan. I stashed my gear in one of the public lockers and took the elevator up to the third floor.

Soon I was buried deep in the pages of a journal from eighteenth-century Halifax.

"Looking for ghosts, are you?"

I looked up, startled by the sound of the voice.

"You're in the wrong place, you know."

The owner of that voice was a short and stocky little man, dressed in a rumpled shirt and a pair of dark, battered work pants. He had the wide-legged solid stance of a sailing man who had only recently come to shore.

"I beg your pardon?" I said.

He smiled. It was a good smile, all crackly and warm like a campfire.

"I said you're in the wrong place if you're looking for ghosts. There's no ghosts here in the Archives. There's nothing here but a lot of facts and figures."

I understood. You run into this sort of an encounter a lot in libraries and archives. Lonely people in search of a little bit of conversation. I quietly decided to humour him. A working artist could use all of the good karma he could gather.

"My name's Garnet," the little man said, "and you've got the look of a man who's looking for ghosts."

I had to smile at that and wondered how he'd guessed.

"Do I know you?" I asked.

"No sir," Garnet said. "But I believe I know you."

I decided that he might have seen my photograph in the newspapers. I'd done a lot of storytelling over the years and had spent a fair bit of my fifteen minutes' worth of fame in the human interest sections of a half dozen local papers.

"Well, as a matter of fact, that's just what I'm here for," I said. "A lot of facts and figures. I'm putting together a collection of Nova Scotian folklore."

"Aye," Garnet said, with as broad a brogue as had ever stepped from the Scottish Highlands. "That's just what I thought. You're looking for ghosts."

It was true enough. I was looking for ghost stories.

"Well you won't find them here," Garnet repeated. "There's no room for ghosts in the Archives. There's no room for mystery in these carefully annotated files and facts and figures. No sir, the only place you'll find a ghost is in stories."

I laughed at that.

"I know that," I said. "I know perfectly well that ghosts aren't real."

"I never said they weren't real; what I said was they're found in stories. That's where they like to live. Stories are what feeds them, like a chowder."

He planted a fist against his hip, a preacher getting set to sermonize. I braced myself for a storm.

"Scientists have yet to tinker a rig so fine that it can calculate the caloric potential of a well-told tale. A handful of good stories can conjure up enough heat to cook up a fine belly-filling chowder. Just add a stone or two, for seasoning."

I grinned at that. "You're preaching to the choir," I said. "I've been telling stories for years. Nova Scotia's got haunted harbours aplenty."

"Go on," Garnet said. "You're too young to call yourself a storyteller."

"Do you think so?" I asked.

"If I'm wrong, prove it," Garnet said.

I recognized a challenge when I saw it.

"Come here," I said. "Let me show you something."

I took him over to the map case and unrolled a great old map of Halifax.

"Look here," I said. "See that beach? It's called Black Rock Beach."

"If you're telling a story," Garnet warned, "don't stop at one. I crave me an earful."

"An earful you shall have."

And I stood there in the heart of the Nova Scotia Archives, and began to tell the tale of Black Rock Beach…

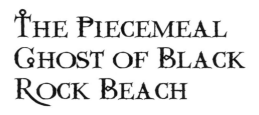

1

THE PIECEMEAL GHOST OF BLACK ROCK BEACH

HALIFAX

A local expert in Halifax legal history told me that Halifax's central gallows were once located at the foot of what is now called George Street, very close to the modern-day ferry terminal. There was also a gallows on the South Common, now the site of the Victoria General Hospital, that was erected back on July 30, 1844, specifically for hanging a gang of convicted pirates.

For a very long time, a set of military gallows, complete with flogging post, stood in the heart of the Citadel Hill parade ground. It was the sight of this gallows and flogging post that prompted Prince Edward's lover and mistress, Julie de Saint-Laurent, to demand that he build her a separate manor, far away from such ugliness. Prince Edward responded by building the famed Prince's Lodge, where footpaths spelled out Julie's name and a brook chuckled merrily down into a heart-shaped pond.

There are still pieces of the public gallows stored at the Old Halifax Courthouse on Spring Garden Road. However, this story concerns another gallows that was erected at Black Rock Beach.

Black Rock Beach is a small open cove at the mouth of the Halifax Harbour, visible from the waterfront parking lot that overlooks Point Pleasant Park. The beach is too shallow to land anything larger than a sloop, but early Halifax settlers found another use for this particular promontory.

Black Rock Beach was the site of one of Halifax's earliest public gallows. The location was chosen because of its visibility. The gallows was a warning sign to sailors on any ship entering the harbour – this is Halifax, don't break the law here.

In 1762, Halifax was a pretty lawless place. France was one year away from ceding Canada to Britain, following their defeat in the Seven Years' War. It was a time of fear and harsh punishments.

✚

A young man stood in the fringe of larch trees overlooking Black Rock Beach, staring at the Black Rock Beach gallows as if he could see his future there. His name was Patrick Tulligan. He was lean, in the way of young men who burn hot and fast. His hair was a wild tangled snarl, caught and knotted by the cold Atlantic wind. He stood in the woods overlooking the beach, staring at the gallows, the timber stark and silhouetted by the setting sun like black burnt bones.

The gallows were a new addition. Before that, the constables had simply dangled criminals from the branch of a standing beach oak. Hangings were more common than you might imagine. One man was hanged for stealing a silver spoon from a downtown tavern where he worked. A year later the spoon was found, beneath the tavern sink where it had fallen.

In fact there were an awful lot of ways to earn yourself a Halifax hanging back in the late 1700s. You could be hanged for offences as varied as murder, treason, rape, manslaughter, arson, highway robbery, polygamy, major theft, firing a gun with intent to injure, cutting a leak hole in a dyke, or unlawful impersonation of another person at a bail hearing. Occasionally, first-time offenders were simply branded with a letter burnt onto the ball of the right thumb. Second-time offenders were automatically hanged.

Patrick stood and stared as any wild young man might, wondering to himself if some day he'd be standing a whole lot closer to that gallows than he'd like.

"You're looking at your doom, Patrick me lad."

Patrick turned. He'd been startled by the sudden voice so close to his ears.

It was Mad Meg, who walked the woods with a rope in her hand, searching for a milk cow who'd run off six years past. She was said to have the evil eye, for her one milky yellow left eye stubbornly stared in the wrong direction.

"Are you looking for your cow then, Meg?" Patrick said, unconcerned.

"Aye. She's not far gone. Just over the hill, I'll wager. I heard her lowing in the woodlands, and I'm close to catching her."

Patrick laughed. Not a cruel laugh, but the laugh of a young man who rarely thinks things through.

"Meg, your cow's been gone for six long years. It's naught but bones and tangleweed, rotting in the dirt somewhere, or chewing fat grass in some farmer's pasture, or rendered down to night soil in the bottom of a thieving beggar's privy."

Meg fixed him with her yellow eye, pointing at the gallows.

"Look long on that swinging collar of hemp, young Patrick, for you'll wear it as a forget-me-knot before the last summer wind blows the first leaf of autumn."

Patrick laughed harder. Meg had been mad long before her cow had wandered off, and few paid her actions any heed. Still, it was whispered that she had the gift of second sight. Some swore she had the evil eye and could jinx anyone she didn't care for.

"You'll hang for three long decades and linger longer, I'll warrant."

He touched his fingertips to his collar, feeling the stubborn knot of his Adam's apple quivering beneath his outstretched thumb. Her words scared him, but he laughed to mask his fear. "Ha!" he scoffed. "How long can a rope hang?"

Meg wrapped her bit of cow-rope about her neck and curtseyed. "Long as memory. Longer than time. Longer than the tail of the wind."

And then she turned and ran like an out-of-control windstorm. In a beat of a bird's wing she was gone, vanished like smoke up a chimney hole.

If he was rattled, Patrick wouldn't show it. He'd hand-hauled codfish and had nearly died in a half a dozen storms at sea. He'd stood and scrapped toe to toe with the biggest sailors this side of the Atlantic. Some he'd beaten and some had beaten him, but none ever dared call him a coward.

He walked the long path back to Halifax with the straps of his gunny sack chafing against his work-hardened shoulders, not realizing how soon it would be that he'd walk this path again and in what manner he would be forced to walk it.

Back then, as now, the streets of Halifax all rolled down to the sea to the harbour front, where the nastiest taverns poured the thinnest of ales and the women's laughter sounded like the clatter of coins. Halifax was a port city. Like today, there were plenty of places for a sailor to spend his money. Folks came and went like the passing of the tides. Everybody expected a profit.

Patrick had a girlfriend named Belinda Marywell, better known as "Belle of the Isle." Belinda was born and raised on McNabs Island. He'd been seeing her for three months, a long time for a lad who'd once sworn he'd never be tied down.

"You'll stand before a preacher, yet," Belinda swore.

"I'll face the hangman first," Patrick allowed.

That night Patrick danced a jig, and not feeling the dark eyes of the innkeeper hanging upon the two of them, stole a kiss from Belinda.

The innkeeper, one Thomas Tanner, was a fat man with an evil disposition. He'd set his heart on the beautiful Belle of the Isle, and vowed she'd be his wife. But Patrick was too tough and had too many friends for Tanner to risk an open confrontation. Besides, there were better ways to get around an obstacle like Patrick.

"You'll dance your next jig on a higher dance floor than this," Tanner swore.

One summer day a ship was robbed and sunk just off Devil's Island. The magistrates searched every tavern for likely suspects. It was an election year, and they were taking no chances. Thomas Tanner was more than glad to help them out. Palms were greased and strings tugged, and Patrick was sentenced for piracy.

Now everyone knew that Patrick, though a wild boy, was certainly no pirate. But the magistrates closed ranks about Tanner's testimony and would hear not one word in young Patrick's defense.

"You shall be whipped at the cart's tail to Black Rock Beach, where you will hang by the neck until death," the judge pronounced, yet all Patrick could hear was the laughter of old Meg taunting him with her prophecy.

The town guard led Patrick down to Black Rock Beach with his hands tied to the back end of an ox cart, whipping him with a great long leather lash. They beat him every step of the way down to the gallows, a guardsman following behind Patrick's cart, laying his whip across Patrick's bare back. Down at the beach they slid the noose about Patrick's throat, snugging it closely to be certain that the knot would snap his neck properly.

Patrick looked wildly about in the crowd that had gathered to watch him drop, searching in vain for the long auburn tresses of his Belle of the Isle. She was nowhere in sight. All that he saw was the crowd, headed by the fat and smirking Thomas Tanner — and high on the slope of the hill looking down on the scene was Mad Meg. She waved her cow rope like a goodbye hankie at young Patrick. The last sound Patrick heard was Meg's laughter rising up like the call of the seagulls over the ever-returning tide.

As Patrick dropped through the trap door, the first leaf of autumn, coaxed by the late August wind, fell from the oak tree above the gallows. Some swore it was a sign that the good luck had run out of Halifax Harbour, but before the sun had fallen the beer mugs were raised in the waterfront taverns and folks forgot about the fate of the young late Patrick Tulligan. Yet across the harbour, Belle of the Isle watched from the shores of McNabs Island, her tears falling down and mixing with the salty Atlantic waves.

After the hanging, the hangman decided that it would be a fine idea to build a cage of iron about the boy's body and let him swing and hang there as a warning to sailors passing into Halifax Harbour.

Patrick hung in his cage with no one but the ravens to keep him company. His bones grew black and fungus stained them blacker still. After a time, even the flies found nothing to feast upon.

The years passed. The Halifax townsfolk forgot Patrick's name. It became a dare for young boys to run up the dark rock and touch the cage. It was whispered that if you got too close to the iron bars, a pair of black withered hands would reach out and grab you and drag you into the cage.

And all this time Belle of the Isle walked the beach of McNabs Island, gazing across at the withered remains of her long-lost lover. She never married, and her long auburn hair ran white as the foam-tossed waves. The passing sailors swore you could hear the sound of the wind running through her hair, the call of her lonely keening haunting the ocean air.

As Patrick's remains slowly rotted, Halifax continued to grow. Houses were built around Black Rock Beach, and those who lived within eyeshot began to complain about the gallows sticking out like a canker in the mouth of the harbour. It seems that old Patrick was bad for real estate values.

The city council decided it would be better to move the gallows to McNabs Island. Being good frugal Scots they dismantled the Black Rock Beach gallows piece by piece and rowed them by dory across the harbour to McNabs Island where they were reassembled. Nearly two hundred years later, in 1966, Thomas Raddall wrote a tale of Peter McNab and his family that centred around these very gallows. He called it "Hangman's Beach," but that is a tale for another time.

The three R's, reduce, reuse, and recycle, were known even then, and the authorities decided to take Patrick with them to a new home on Hangman's Beach. But the bones that had hung for thirty long years were brittle with age. By the time the cage reached the dory, Patrick had fallen to pieces. His bones, broken and scattered too fine and too far to bother picking up, were left upon the beach for the crabs to pick over.

Even now, the fishermen say that on long lonely August nights you can hear Belle walking the McNabs Island beach line, calling out soft and low to her long-lost lover – "Patrick, oh, Patrick."

And on certain August nights, a figure of a young man has been seen stooping and bending on Black Rock Beach, picking up pieces of something from the ground.

So if you're out there, on Black Rock Beach when the moon is hanging over the waters like a fat rotted pumpkin, and some strange fellow walks up to you and asks "Can you give me a hand?," I believe I'd run if I were you.

2

THE RESTLESS SPIRITS OF DEVIL'S ISLAND

DEVIL'S ISLAND

I first set foot on Devil's Island a long time ago. At the time, the only residents were a caretaker, his wife, and a large friendly German Shepherd by the name of Thor. The caretaker was an artist, and his wife an author, so both of them enjoyed the seclusion that their choice of neighbourhood provided. I was spellbound by the tangible mysteries that lurked on this small forgotten island with its oh-so-intriguing name. The island sits just beyond the mouth of Halifax Harbour about two kilometres southeast of McNabs Island. Several years after my visit, Devil's Island was sold to a private buyer. There isn't a single living soul upon it these days. The automated lighthouse is the only sign that life ever existed there.

But there are many souls — and many stories — that linger there still.

✠

Devil's Island is not named as such on many old maps. In 1758 it is mentioned as being within the boundaries of the newly formed Halifax Township. The town's limits were decreed to extend from the western head of Bedford Basin and across the northerly head of St. Margaret's Bay, including Cornwallis Island, Webb's Island, and Rous Island. Rous, now known as Devil's Island, was named after its first owner, Captain John Rous. Prior to that it was some-times called Wood Island, for the stand of trees upon it.

There are as many ghost tales of Devil's Island as there are names for this tiny little speck of rock. Sadly, like many a Nova Scotian name, the true etymology of Devil's Island has been lost in the misty regions between myth and barely-recorded history. An early article in the July 6, 1901 edition of the Dartmouth *Patriot* tells us that the name "Devil's Island" came from the previous owner, a Monsieur Duvall. For a time folks apparently referred to the island as Duvall's Island, but as the depredations of the Maritimer's notoriously relaxed tongue and innate sense of cheek-iness took over, the island came to be known as Devil's Island.

The island is a barren patch, with nary a branch nor twig upon it. But there was once a small forest and a town consisting of eighteen dwellings and a school of sorts that passed through the nurturing guidance of four separate schoolmasters. It is said that an untimely forest fire ravaged the island during World War I, when most of the young men had left; they never returned. The wee island settled into the fog of mystery and the depredation of eventual neglect.

Folks often tell of how back in the early 1900s Dave Henneberry and Ned Edwards saw what looked to be a large white barrel floating in the surf. "It's the devil's treasure," swore Henneberry. "Every seven years it surfaces for a wee bit of sunshine, strictly to tease the angels, and then it sinks straight to the bottom."

"Should we take a shot at it?" asked Ned, raising his rifle. "Maybe if we put a hole in it we'll slow it down some."

"And risk riling the devil himself? I should say not."

But then Dave, demonstrating a strange Island-born perversity, bent and picked up a beach stone and winged it fair and square directly at the large white barrel. The stone made a strange thunking sound, and the white barrel slid back into the ocean as if it had never been there.

Why did he do it? For luck? For spite? Nobody knows, but the very next morning Henneberry was found in his rowboat, drifting far too close to the position where he and Ned had first spotted the pale white casket. Henneberry was drowned with his head and shoulders hanging over the side of the boat, as if he'd simply fallen asleep while staring at something deep beneath the water. Was he a victim of foul play, or did he die because he tampered with the devil's treasure box? Only time and the tide truly know and neither is in the habit of telling many tales, however Henneberry's wife swore that on the night Henneberry died, she heard the clomping of his big rubber boots and later found his wet tracks on the floorboards of the hallway.

In later years another generation of Henneberrys moved in to the old family house. No sooner had they moved in, but their baby died in its crib. Such an untimely death was fairly common in that day and age, but some folks claimed that the Henneberrys were cursed because they lived on Devil's Island. Their house was later rumoured to be haunted by the sounds of a baby crying, loud and eerie in the middle of the night. Worn to weariness by grief and terror, the family eventually tore down the house. Wood, being in short supply, quickly found a use; the lumber of the old Henneberry house was scavenged and recycled by kin and neighbours alike.

But those who used the wood soon learned to rue their Scotian frugality. Every house that laid a plank of Henneberry wood in its framing was reported to be haunted either by the sound of Henneberry's sloshing rubber boots or the weeping wail of a dying infant. Those who burned the wood swore they heard the sound of a baby screaming in the heart of the flames.

To this day it is said that the descendants of the Henneberry family refuse to set foot on the shores of Devil's Island. Passing fishermen have sometimes seen a baby's cradle floating in the water but as soon as they move their boats close enough to see it clearly, the cradle seems to slide into the water and quickly vanish.

3

THE TALE OF THE YOUNG TEAZER

MAHONE BAY

Nova Scotia is a peninsula and there are very few locations within its borders where you can stand more than fifty miles from the ocean, so what book of Nova Scotian ghost stories would be complete without a tale of a phantom ship?

There are quite a few ghost ship stories to be found in Nova Scotia, so many that one wonders why all of these fabled ghost ships haven't been written up by the Coast Guard as a maritime traffic hazard.

There is the well-reported phantom ship that sails up and down the Northumberland Strait, the empty drifting *Mary Celeste*, and Captain Kidd's famous treasure ship. Yet the Mahone Bay tale of the *Young Teazer* has long been a favourite of mine.

✠

Back in the early 1800s privateering was a profitable but dangerous profession. Privateering was a barely legal form of piracy. A
captain would apply for a letter of commission from his monarch
and/or ruler, and then would set out to capture every enemy vessel he could.

Every captured vessel and sometimes its crew, if they could
be easily taken, were brought in to the naval commission of the
pirate's home country for a suitable reward. These captured ships
would be converted and put to use in the fleet, sometimes as privateers themselves. Ships were swapped back and forth like bub-
ble gum baseball trading cards.

Such was the case of the *Young Teazer*. Originally the property of a Spanish slaver, she was captured and sold at Halifax in
1811. She was refitted and then served as a packet vessel, sailing
between Liverpool and London, under the very practical name of
the *Liverpool Packet*.

When the War of 1812 broke out, the *Liverpool Packet* was
refitted yet again and received a privateer's commission from
the British government. As a privateer, this small, fast fifty-four
by eighteen-and-a-half foot vessel was very successful. She single-
handedly captured more than a dozen enemy vessels with the
help of five cannon and a crew of forty-five. Eventually, though,
she was captured by the American vessel, *Thomas*. She was sold
at auction again and renamed the *Young Teazer*.

Are you keeping score? So far the *Young Teazer* has been a
Spanish ship, a British commercial vessel, a British privateer, and
now an American privateer.

Her new master, young lieutenant Frederick Johnson, took
command of her in 1813, directly following his capture and

release by the British forces, and therein lies the heart of the tale. You see, Lieutenant Johnson was captured by the British with his previous vessel and had signed a parole note promising that he would return to his home town and never take up arms against the British forces again. Yet no sooner had he returned to Maine than he signed on as the master of the *Young Teazer*.

Some might think poorly of young master Johnson for breaking his signed word, but the fact was that he had signed the parole promise under duress. Besides, he was a career military man and knew no other trade. At this time in history, if you wanted to be a member of the American fleet, you had best be resigned to fighting the British and the Canadians.

So off he sailed, but he might as well have stayed at home. His bad luck hadn't changed a whit. No sooner had he set sail than a pair of British warships caught him and the *Young Teazer* just outside of Mahone Bay Harbour, on June 26, 1813.

In an effort to escape his pursuers, Lieutenant Johnson turned the *Young Teazer* into Mahone Bay Harbour, hoping to take shelter behind Great Tancook Island. This should have been an easy trick, given the many islands that clustered and cluttered up the waters of the harbour.

The *Young Teazer* fired a blast from her cannon and turned into the wind. The British bracketed him with their own cannon fire. Johnson was outnumbered and outmaneuvered, cut off at every turn.

Not wanting to hang for breaking his parole promise, Lieutenant Johnson set fire to the *Young Teazer* in a desperate attempt to escape. He hoped that he and his men might row out of the reach of the blaze in their lifeboats and escape in the smoke and ensuing confusion. Alas, he had forgotten to take into consideration the ample cargo of gunpowder the *Young Teazer* had been carrying with future sea battles in mind. As the flames reached the powder kegs, the entire ship went up in an explosion that rocked the shores and rattled the window panes of the nearby town of Mahone Bay.

There were few, if any, survivors aboard the doomed *Young Teazer*. The records regarding this matter vary wildly. It is a fact that the body of Lieutenant Frederick Johnson was lost to the careless tossing of the waves.

The fire-gutted hull of the *Young Teazer*, scorched clear down to the waterline, was towed into Chester Bay on the following day and sold off as salvage. What was left of the hull was used as the foundation of what is now the Rope Loft Restaurant in downtown Chester. The keelson, a timber fastened above and parallel to the keel of the ship for additional strength, was used to construct a large wooden cross that is now a part of St. Stephen's Church in Chester.

To this day, residents and passing ships claim to have seen the ghost of the *Young Teazer* sailing through the mist and the moonlight of Mahone Bay Harbour, just rounding the hook of Great Tancook Island. The hot tongues of a ghostly raging fire are seen licking at the ragged sails, and the spirits of the restless dead sailors still hang and burn in the rigging. Pragmatic party-poopers point out that this is nothing more than the light of the moon filtered through the nimbus clouds and night fog. Other wiser folk have declared that the vision is nothing more than the silhouetted mast of a tall spruce tree seen through evening fog as the sun sets, but I've never been one to listen too closely to practical thinkers. Ask any old-time sailor and he'll tell you one truth: every ship has her own soul, a spirit as specific and individual as fingerprints.

I think the *Young Teazer* had been transformed so many times that she simply looked at her sinking as one more refit. Now she prowls the mists and the darkness of the Mahone Bay water, faithfully keeping her final station.

Nearly two hundred years later, Mahone Bay holds an annual Wooden Boat Festival, whose highlight is the reenactment of the burning of the *Young Teazer*. Two local vessels play the part of the British ships and a third takes the role of the *Young Teazer*. Shotgun cannons and a road flare help simulate the gun duel and the subsequent fire. This reenactment is followed by the symbolic burning of a scale model *Young Teazer* and afterwards, if weather permits, you can count on a rousing display of fireworks.

Visit Mahone Bay someday if you have the chance. You might be surprised to see the *Young Teazer*, sailing through the misty waters. Or perhaps you'll happen upon the wandering ghost of Lieutenant Frederick Johnson, still seeking to evade British justice, haunting the dockyards and the shoreline of the harbour.

Don't be scared; I'm only teasing.

4

OLD NICK
IS RINGING
HIS BELL

LUNENBURG

Someone told me a bit of this tale at a
Christmas party, but by the time I'd gotten home, the memory was lost in a soft
fog of festivities, food, and too much winter ale. I spent some research time at the
Archives, and a whole month scouring
the used bookstores for old texts. This
search brought me two more sides of this
story – each imperfect, each incomplete.
I have taken it upon myself to weld the
two sides together and I've come up with
something that sounds a little like this.

✠

In the mid-1700s Nova Scotia was billed
as a promised land of milk and moose
meat. Ruthless government agents travelled through Northern Europe enticing

unwary settlers to pack up and venture across the Atlantic to settle there.

"Land for every man," they swore. "Soil that parts like sea water before the plow. Fresh game and fish for the asking. Room for everyone and a chance for a brand new beginning." Such were the promises made for money; the land agents received a bounty from the British government for every colonist they managed to seduce. However, as this mixed bag of European settlers arrived in Halifax, they were told a completely different story. Halifax had been built for the British, they were told. There was no room for Dutch, German, or Swiss settlers.

So it was that in the early summer of 1753, a group of fifteen hundred German, Swiss, and Dutch settlers sailed out of Halifax and into Malagash Bay. They settled on the shores of what would later be known as Lunenburg, determined to make a fresh start for themselves. They swore to build a new life on this cold and unfriendly shoreline.

They were harassed by the coming winter, the harsh conditions of the untilled land, and the depredations of local Mi'kmaq riled up by the French, who had their own notions of who should or should not be allowed to take root in this brand new world.

Everybody wanted a piece of this landscape, yet by the early 1760s France had surrendered the entire country to the British and the settlers had made peace treaties with the local natives and got down to the serious business of building a home.

The settlers took root mostly on the coastline, which provided a ready-made escape route. The ocean was their friend and if there was ever any sign of trouble they could simply sail away.

But Nicholas Spohr was of tougher stock. He hunted upriver, looking for a patch of land far from the crowded towns to call his own. In Germany he'd been a landless peasant, and had harboured dreams of owning his own estate.

He found his dreams made manifest far up the LaHave River on the shores of a large horseshoe-shaped cove. Here, in the wooded darkness of the Nova Scotia forest, Nicholas found an entire abandoned settlement. There were docks leading out into the river and a large clearing, containing a great blockhouse with cannons still mounted in their swivels. There was a large warehouse that looked to have once served as a church on Sundays, with a large black belfry and a great iron bell mounted therein. He could see the bell from the shore, swaying softly in the evening wind.

How long had this settlement stood here? Had it been abandoned by the French during their flight from the province? Perhaps the original inhabitants had been wiped out by a plague or a massacre. Nicholas didn't know.

He warily explored the deserted settlement, not finding a single sign of the original inhabitants. Who were they? That they had been craftsmen was evident: the buildings were well constructed. Several gardens were carefully laid out and showed signs of recent tending. The houses were unlocked and fully stocked with all manner of furniture, clothing, silverware and many household necessities.

Where had the owners gone? If they'd fled the British advance, why hadn't they taken their belongings with them? If they'd died of disease or been killed, where were their remains? If they had been massacred, why hadn't their killers taken any of their belongings?

It was a mystery, but a blessing for Nicholas that he simply could not ignore. Here was an estate for the taking. He was a landowner.

He hurried back to Lunenburg, not telling a soul of his sudden great luck. The blockhouse was apparently forgotten to all, and Nicholas intended for it to remain so. He travelled to Halifax by boat and asked the British authorities for a grant of the land located seven miles up the LaHave River.

The authorities didn't ask any questions. It seemed they had no knowledge of the previous settlement, either. They were more than eager to settle the untamed Nova Scotian interior wilderness. And why not? The sooner it was securely settled, the sooner the government could begin imposing taxes. They happily gave Nicholas a grant for one thousand acres of untouched land in and about the little horseshoe-shaped harbour that is now known as Horseshoe Cove.

Nicholas hastened back to Lunenburg and quickly moved his family from their temporary town dwelling up the LaHave River to take possession of the abandoned blockhouse.

Within a year Nicholas began displaying the effects of his sudden good fortune. He discarded his sensible homespun jacket, his wool stockings and trousers, even his battered felt hat and wooden sabots. He began dressing in the fancy garments he'd found in the abandoned houses of the settlement. He took to riding and spent much of his time wandering and admiring his lands and his buildings.

Instead of working the land for a living, Nicholas amassed a small fortune by selling off firewood cut by his sons. Nicholas, a landowner now, considered himself far too dignified for such menial labor. One wonders what his sons might have thought about this.

Nicholas saved his peasant attire for the times when he would have to travel to Lunenburg. He only wore his fancy duds within the security of his own landholdings. Perhaps he feared the thought of other people learning of his good fortune, or perhaps he was afraid that they might see through his pretense and laugh at him. In any case, as soon as he returned to the sanctuary of his own lands, off would come the peasant garb, and he would immediately change back into his fancy wear, sometimes as he crossed the border of his own land. Many a hunter has told the tale of seeing old Nicholas tugging on his silk trousers in the heart of the darkened Nova Scotia forest.

Every Sunday Nicholas would ring the blockhouse bell, thanking God for his good fortune. You could hear it, clear to Lunenburg, tolling long and low.

All went well for many a year. Nicholas lived out his charade, relying on the wealth his family's efforts provided. He occasionally carried some of the valuables from the settlement to be sold off at Halifax. He never sold any of the clothing. He couldn't part with any of his lucky finery.

Then one night Nicholas was awoken by the sounds of a great drum beating in the heart of his richest woodlot. "Someone is stealing my timber," he shouted to his family. He dressed himself in a combination of his finest garments and peasant wear, whatever was closest at hand. With a loaded pistol in his hand, and armed with the indomitable sense of his own self-righteousness, he strode boldly into the forest depths, following the sound of the beating drum.

Within a half an hour Nicholas found himself in the heart of a vast Mi'kmaq gathering. Believing that his right of ownership granted by the Halifax authorities would somehow impress the Mi'kmaq, Nicholas brandished his loaded pistol and ordered the group to leave his lands.

Nicholas was inches away from his own death. Even though the tribes had long ago made peace with the British, it was still considered most unsociable to wave loaded weaponry in a stranger's face. Only the fact that the Mi'kmaq thought him more funny than dangerous saved his life. They took his pistol and turned him out into the darkness.

Nicholas brooded through long days and nights, hearing the Mi'kmaq ceremonial drum beating in his very own woodlot. Three days later when the Mi'kmaq left their ceremonial grounds, Nicholas moved in with all of his sons and cut that section bare. He even deigned to pick up an axe himself. He worked from sun-up to sundown, tearing his favourite pilfered silk shirt in his effort to make that section of land absolutely inhospitable. Nicholas hauled the felled timber to Lunenburg and had it loaded on a ship, and he personally saw to the delivery in Halifax. It was his best load yet. He returned home to Lunenburg with his pockets jingling and he grinned with the sweet taste of revenge.

His grin faded when he returned to his estate and found that his entire family had been murdered. Even his dog had been gutted. The furniture had been broken up and his fine clothing torn and burnt. He knelt over the ashes and howled like a gut-shot wolf. They say that the townsfolk heard his screams all the way back into Lunenburg; if they didn't hear the scream they certainly heard the bell tolling long both day and night.

Eventually Nicholas wandered back into the settlement of Lunenburg, a shadow of his former self. His fine clothing was torn into rags upon his back. His eyes were dulled with madness.

The settlers rallied to his cause and gathered a hunting party of stout German and Dutch farmers and sailors armed with muskets and pistols. They managed to hunt up several Mi'kmaq, hanging four of them in front of the site of the massacre at Horseshoe Cove. Doubtless many of these Mi'kmaq were innocent, and a lot of blood was needlessly spilled, but the townsfolk felt that justice had prevailed. They shipped two of the Mi'kmaq survivors to Halifax for trial. One died in prison and one escaped.

For a time Nicholas Spohr lived alone in the town of Lunenburg, getting drunk every night with what was left of the profits of his last wood sale. He swore that he would never return to the accursed blockhouse at Horseshoe Cove.

Then one moonlit night he disappeared, walking into the Nova Scotian woods. Most of the townsfolk figured he'd been drunk and had simply wandered off, but a few wiser folk knew better. They searched for three days and finally found him outside of the blockhouse, prostrate upon his wife's grave, dead from hunger, exposure, and the ravages of grief.

They buried him there, outside of the blockhouse that had promised him so much happiness. For many a year the site was shunned by whites and Mi'kmaq alike. Yet in the restless nights of autumn, when the wind is dancing with the clouds and talking of the snow that soon will fly, the story goes that you can hear the sound of an iron bell tolling a low and mournful dirge, even though the blockhouse has long since vanished. Local folks who hear it, even today, will simply shrug their shoulders and walk on: Old Nicholas is ringing his bell and walking a lonely vigil through a woodlot that has never grown back quite right.

5

The
Ghost-Hunter's
Whistling Ghost

LIVERPOOL

In her 1968 collection *Bluenose Magic*, Helen Creighton tells of a lot of different ways that you can slay a witch or rid yourself of a ghost. Silver will do it; water will too. So will fire and salt. I've since heard the following old story of a rogue witch-hunter who used just such a technique to make a small living, although I have reason to believe that his motives were less than silvery pure.

✠

Back in the early 1800s in the Liverpool area, there lived an old man named Hank O'Hallorhan. Hank was a bandy-legged fellow, not half as old as he looked, but as lazy as a fat frog wallowing in the bottom of a mossy well. Hank used to be a sailor, but no ship would have him for very long because of his bad habit of whistling too much. Hank was a nervous little man who found relief through whistling, something no sailor could stand due to the old superstition that an idle whistler could just as easily whistle up a storm as a tune. So Hank became a hunter, though of an unusual sort. He'd go from town to town and enter someone's house, making sniffing sounds and saying, "I smell a ghost," or "I smell a witch."

If he claimed to smell a ghost he'd fire a charge of black powder up the chimney flue to frighten the evil spirits away. If it was a witch he was chasing, he'd beg a dime that he'd cut up into slices to fire up the chimney, because everyone knew that silver was the only thing that could slay a witch. He'd beg a dime at every house, but would only slice up the one; even a witch hunter needs to make some kind of living.

One day he showed up at an old woman's house and swore he could smell a witch. Actually what he'd smelled was a brace of freshly baked apple pies cooling by the windowsill. Hank figured on making a bit of money and perhaps a piece of pie or two. He walked up to the front porch, whistling like a flock of lovesick canaries.

The old woman, whose name was Annie Tuckins, fixed Hank with a hard, sharp stare.

"Damn a man who whistles," she said. "He's either got something on his mind, or absolutely nothing at all."

"Oh grandmother," Hank said, figuring he'd get farther by talking politely. "I smell a witch in your chimney. She'll cast a spell on your baking for certain sure. Would you have a dime that I might use to banish her?"

The old woman looked up from her baking, half-amused by O'Hallorhan's gall and half-bothered by his unasked-for interruption.

"Only a dime? Witches come cheap in these parts," she said. "And how much would it cost me to banish you?"

"You may laugh," O'Hallorhan replied. "But I tell you this true. There are witches in every corner of this sainted province. They're easier to find than toads in a peat bog. Standing in the shadow of every black cat is a witch in waiting. They might be your neighbour or they might live a half a dozen counties away. There's no telling where a witch'll turn up, if she puts her mind to it."

"So how can you tell if one is a witch or not?" the old woman asked, playing along with O'Hallorhan's banter.

"Oh, there's many a way you can tell if a person is a witch. For instance, if you lay your broom across your front doorway, the witch cannot cross it."

The old woman snorted. "It sounds to me like a perfectly good way to trip yourself going into your house."

O'Hallorhan laughed easily. An acre of brooms could not trip up such a sly-talking, fast-thinking man as he.

"And a young woman such as yourself would jig lightly over a palisade of brooms, now would she not? Heel and toe, you're a light stepper, like the fog running in from the bay."

"Flatterer. So here's a piece of silver and that'll buy your trick, won't it?"

O'Hallorhan palmed the old woman's coin and pulled out one of his own, a tin disc he'd bartered from a tinker. He cut the tin disc up with his case knife and carefully loaded the fragment into his musket, after filling the gun with powder.

He tamped the makeshift metal shot down securely with his ramrod.

"You ought to oil that rod before it rusts," the old woman pointed out.

"It rams as straight as the day it was first hammered out," Hank said with a wink.

He cocked back the hammer, inserted the firing cap, and let fly, firing the homemade ball of tin straight into the old woman's fireplace. The cheap powder he'd used smoked the kitchen out.

"There you go, good grandmother. It's done and done. The witch will bother you no more."

The old woman laughed. "She never bothered me in the first place. So off with you then, you have my silver and my blessing. I'll count it an experience and thank God for it tonight in my prayers. It's reckoned fine good luck to help a beggar."

O'Hallorhan bristled at the word "beggar," but he said nothing about it. He had eyes for the old woman's apple pie. "It's better luck to feed one, Granny. Why don't you carve me off a slice of that hot apple pie, and a wee nugget of cheese if you have it?"

The old woman's humour hardened. "Be off with you. You've palmed my dime and fired that wee bit of metal you thought to pass for silver and you've fouled up my kitchen with your dirty cheap powder." She grabbed her broom up from the floor. "Leave this house now, or I'll put this broom to a better use than tripping up witches."

O'Hallorhan wouldn't have it. "I'll have that pie before I go. I can still smell the witch, and she needs another blast or two."

"You'll have the end of this broom, and you'll be picking splinters for a fortnight," the old woman said.

O'Hallorhan looked her in the eye. "Well I'm walking that way," he said, pointing towards Liverpool. "And there's a lot of houses between here and midnight. It'd be a shame if word got around of how I smelled a witch in your house and you wouldn't let me smoke it out." He had her then. She knew the trouble that O'Hallorhan could start for her.

"Take the pie and be done with it," she told him.

But O'Hallorhan would have nothing to do with that. In his eyes he had to earn the pie fair and square. So he loaded up his gun, but in his hurry and cheapness he slid in a plain lead shot, once again keeping the dime for the silver.

He fired a blast up the chimney but it ricocheted off the chimney stone, and struck O'Hallorhan square in the heart, killing him stone dead. The old woman was sorry to see O'Hallorhan dead, but not sorry enough to forget about retrieving his pilfered silver.

For years afterwards, the old woman would hear a whistle up the chimney flue, and even though most folks swore it was nothing more than a hole left by O'Hallorhan's shot, the old woman swore it was the ghost of the old witch-hunter.

"Shut up, you old whistling crook," she would yell, "or I'll fire a whole barrel full of silver up that flue and finish you good and proper."

6

THE JORDAN FALLS FORERUNNER

JORDON FALLS

Storytelling isn't like writing. You've got to put a little more of yourself into it when you're sitting there staring at your audience across the flicker of a campfire or into the glare of stage lights. So I hope you'll forgive me if I talk a little of my own life now.

I was raised in the woods of Northern Ontario, high in the shield country, about twenty miles north of Sudbury in a little town called Capreol. My mom and dad had married a little too early and went their separate ways, and my brother Dan and I were raised by our grandparents. Dan is still out there in Capreol, working for the CNR. My mom went back home to Yarmouth, Nova Scotia, and Dad eventually moved out west to Blairmore, Alberta.

Being a working man, Dad had little time to travel, and neither did I.

I can count the number of days my father and I had any chance to speak with each other. He once travelled to Nova Scotia for two weeks to come see me. We talked as best we could, shared a beer or two, and tried to make up for the years that had been left behind.

He was a lonely man, I think, but happy nonetheless. He'd found a good woman who put up with his lonely ways. He became the president of the Blairmore Legion and was responsible for the building of a brand new legion hall.

He died at age fifty-eight of a sudden heart attack. I received the telephone call late at night. "Your dad's had a heart attack," Lila said. I remember thinking how my grandfather had lived through three such heart attacks. "He'll have to slow down," I said. Only it was a little late for that. The old reaper had already slowed Dad down for good.

I flew out to Blairmore to see him one last time. I touched his cheek in the coffin, cold and ruddy from a life spent working outdoors.

The night before my dad died I dreamed of him. In my dream we were sitting in the living room I'd grown up in and we were watching an old western on the television. We talked and got along, as if time had not passed. And then he turned to me and said, "I'll be going now."

I do not talk of this much, but that is how it happened. A night later I stood in my kitchen receiving the hardest telephone call I've ever had to take. Was it a coincidence? Maybe, but I tend to believe that my father's spirit came to me in my dream to make peace and to tell me to hang onto my memories of him in any way I could.

✠

In the winter of 1888, a great blizzard ravaged the eastern coast of the United States and the Maritimes, dumping over four feet of snow and paralyzing transportation, yet there were far more chilling events about to transpire.

In the tiny village of Jordan Falls, just outside of Shelburne, Ephraim Doane awoke in his bedroom, screaming as if the devil were at his very door.

"Abandon ship!" he called out, sitting upright in his bed, terrifying his young wife Mabel.

She rose and made them a cup of tea, allowing Ephraim to catch his breath.

"What's wrong?" she asked.

"I've had a terrible dream."

Now Mabel was descended from a long line of highland women, and she knew enough about the power of dreams. Spirits talked to you in dreams, and gods and devils walked hand in hand through the mist-ridden foothills of sleep.

"Tell me about it," she said to him.

"We were out at sea in the midst of a terrible gale. The ship was heel-toeing like a step dancer's boot. I looked out into the roiled-up waters and saw your eyes looking at me, and then somewhere high above my head I heard the mainmast snap and fall."

Mabel sat and sipped her tea. She knew what a forerunner was. To dream of death in such a way meant death was certainly headed straight for you.

"You must stay home," she told him. "Nothing but bad luck will come of such a dream."

Ephraim Doane was a stubborn Nova Scotian man, and Mabel knew that arguing with him was about as productive as ordering the wind to rest from its constant blowing.

"There's fish out there for the catching," Ephraim said, "and these bills won't be paying themselves."

"Well then, wear this," Mabel said, pulling her grandmother's silver crucifix from her neck.

"I can't take this," Ephraim said. "It belonged to your grandmother."

"Bring it back to me, then," Mabel fiercely said, clasping the tiny silver cross about her husband's neck.

So the next morning before the crows had even gotten out of bed, Ephraim Doane pulled on his two pairs of socks and his gum rubber boots and made the journey down to the pier. His ship sailed that morning, heading for the fishing grounds, but Mabel refused to watch it sail away.

There's a stillness that seems to hush the very air just before a big storm rushes in on the sea or the shore. You can feel it as the sky seems to hold its breath in dread of what is about to come.

On board Ephraim's ship, the captain warned, "Batten the hatches and make fast all lines. There's a heavy guster coming in hard and strong."

The watchful crew had already begun setting about the necessary preparations. It was good to hear their instinctive certainty confirmed by the captain's unmistakable orders. When all of the preparations had been tended to and all of the loose hatches made fast and the lines tied and retied there was nothing left to do but to hold on tight and see if the ship could outlive the blow.

Ephraim wasn't worried. He'd been a sailor and fisherman his whole life and he had long ago sworn on the Southern Cross that he'd be buried on the dry land. Yet the other night's dream kept bothering him. It haunted him so much that when he heard the mainmast snap he looked straight up, hoping beyond hope that he was still swimming in the depths of his nightmare.

All hands went down with the ship. The December waters in the Atlantic are cold enough to freeze the very blood in a man's veins. The storm took everyone; not a single survivor remained.

Back on land, Mabel had no such doubts. She knew what a forerunner meant. Just as soon as Ephraim left that morning, she cried for a full half hour. Then, deciding that her husband would suffer through more than his share of salt water and sorrow, she busied herself brushing off his best jacket and pants and preparing for the bad news she felt certain would come.

Three days and three nights passed without a sign of Ephraim's vessel. Everyone in the town presumed that the ship had sunk without a trace. Such events were common in coastal towns.

On the fourth morning they found him washed ashore, still clinging to all that remained of the mainmast. Tucked in his frozen hands was Mabel's silver crucifix.

He'd come home to his wife, as he'd promised, bringing her crucifix home, as he'd likewise promised, and he was buried on dry land as he'd sworn so long ago upon the stars of the Southern Cross.

7

As Pale as Ice and as Hard as Stone

MUD ISLAND

About eighty kilometres southwest of Shelburne, you will be certain to notice three ill-formed islands located in the heart of Lobster Bay and called Seal, Mud, and John's.

Seal is named for the great herd of gray seals that make their home there at certain times of the year. I really don't know who John was. Perhaps a sailor who drowned close to the island, or an early settler. Perhaps it was once the site of a convenient outdoor privy.

But I can tell you about Mud Island, holder of the murky secret of the cold stone woman.

Back in 1833, the brig *Victory* set sail for New York City carrying a cargo of Cape

Breton granite. The brig was helmed by one George Card of Campobello, New Brunswick and had a crew of seven: five sturdy sailors, a cook, and his assistant, a young red-headed girl named Maggie Flynn.

The weather was calm that day and they'd travelled far and the captain decided to drop anchor in the sheltered lee of Mud Island.

That night, following a long calm, one of the worst nor'easter gales on record slammed into the still waters of Lobster Bay, lashing her full fury on the unwary Victory.

The captain, fearing that the force of the storm would tear the ship from her anchor and turn her, ordered the ship's cook and young Maggie Flynn into a dory.

Now it might sound like a strange notion, sending a person from a large and sturdy brig to the dubious shelter of a dory in the heart of a gale, but the captain knew what he was doing. A dory was an awfully hard thing to sink. If the weather was bad enough, the sailors would seal the dory up with canvas, and they would ride the storm out, hunkered down in its belly, bobbing along like a cork in the waves.

The waves were rough as young Maggie stepped into the dory. She nearly slipped as her feet caught on a poorly laid rope.

"Sit down!" a sailor called, but the sea was too loud for him to be clearly heard. As Maggie turned toward the sailor, a great wave smashed up against the side of the dory and threw her into the water.

One sailor jumped down into the dory to try and rescue her. He could see her in the water, tossed like a child in a blanket game. "Grab hold!" he shouted, reaching his arm out over the water.

He looked back once, hoping for a little help from the rest of the crew, but the other sailors were far too busy trying to keep the Victory afloat.

"Come on!" he shouted.

Maggie managed to hook one arm up about the bow of the dory. The young sailor worked his way down to her. He could see her face, pale and staring like a death mask, from the heart of the storm-tossed Atlantic and the sight moved him. He worked his way forward and tried to grab on to Maggie's arm. Another wave rocked the dory, the sailor plunged into the angry waters. Dressed far more heavily than Maggie, he sank like three-day-old biscuit. The dory broke against the ship's hull and Maggie was lost.

The storm turned the *Victory* over and stove her in two like a rotted barrel. The captain and the entire crew were lost to the angry waters. After the storm eased up, searchers found the hulk of the ship grounded in the mud flats surrounding Mud Island. The corpses of the five dead sailors, covered in dead eel grass, were strewn around the wreckage of the *Victory*, like the points on a compass. The captain was still clinging to the wheel, his dead hands frozen hard to the spokes.

They buried the sailors on the shore of Mud Island. The ground was wet and soft for the digging. Shortly after the last grave was dug, a searcher stumbled across the body of poor Maggie Flynn, lying face upward in the shallow water, her arm still hooked about the broken bow stem of the ship's dory. Her face was as pale as ice, her flesh as hard as stone.

This hardness was far more than simple rigor mortis. Young Maggie was petrified, like a hod of sculpting clay that had hardened in the heat of the sun, as if her flesh had turned to granite.

Some said it was something in the water; others claimed it was something in the mud, while still others blamed it on the unseasonable chill of the cold gray Atlantic waters. Whatever the reason, the body of young Maggie Flynn was as cold, hard, and pale as any marble church sculpture.

At first the sailors who had found her were afraid to touch her strangely altered flesh.

"We'll turn to stone ourselves," one swore. "Don't touch her."

"It's devil's work," another said.

"She is a Maritime woman who has died at sea," their leader pointed out. "She'll get a decent Christian burial, even if she was turned to hot burning glass."

They quickly fell to their work and in a short time had churned the dirt deep enough to lay poor Maggie safely at rest.

They ended the day at a local tavern where ale loosened their tired tongues.

"Digging is thirsty work, and an ale or two will wash the taint of grave dirt from our throats," said one.

"Aye," agreed another, "and a tot of rum will wash the taint of ale from our lips."

It goes without saying that drinking leads to gossip as sure as all rivers lead home to the sea. Soon enough the entire tavern had heard the tale of Mud Island's petrified woman. Before too long, a boatload of drunken sailors were rowing themselves out to see the petrified remains of poor Maggie Flynn. They dug her up and had their fill of staring, burying her back down in a careless and shallow manner.

Soon word got around to the whole town that a stone woman had been buried in the dirt of Mud Island. Entertainment like that was clearly hard to pass up in nineteenth-century rural Nova Scotia and soon the midnight boat tours and excavations became a regular event. Curiosity seekers from far and wide stole out to take a look at the woman made of stone.

Finally, an old couple who lived on the island took it upon themselves to dig up Maggie Flynn's grave and rebury her in an undisclosed spot. They said it was the only Christian thing to do, but it wouldn't be surprising if they had had enough of the nightly rambles of young drunken thrill-seekers.

It has been said by more than a few storytellers that if you pass over a certain part of Mud Island you will feel a chill in your bones, as if you'd climbed into a meat locker. I don't know about that, but I do believe that somewhere on Mud Island, about fifteen miles from Clarke's Harbour, the mortal remains of one Maggie Flynn are lying beneath the soft black dirt, as pale as ice and as hard as stone.

8

The Captain's House at Yarmouth

YARMOUTH

I was born and raised in northern Ontario. At the age of seventeen I took it into my head to travel from my home to Yarmouth to meet my mother, whom I hadn't seen since I was a young child of three. I lived in Yarmouth for most of a summer, working at the IMO fish plant and the Domtec cotton mill, and very quickly I fell in love with the Atlantic coast.

I can remember landing in Halifax and getting off the plane, expecting to see the ocean. I'd forgotten to adjust my watch for the time change, and I missed my connecting flight to Yarmouth. So I walked out of the airport, planning to hike to Yarmouth. How far could it be? Nova Scotia was such a tiny spot on the map; certainly it couldn't take more than an hour or so to cross on foot.

I walked as far as the first mileage sign that told me the true distance separating Halifax and Yarmouth and eventually, I found my way to a bus.

While I was celebrating my eighteenth birthday, my brother and sisters decided it was time I heard the following tale. Unfortunately, having just attained the legal drinking age, I didn't remember much more than a snippet of the story. When I was putting this collection together, I decided to hunt this story up and after much research, I tick-tacked this version of it together.

✠

The old Stott house, also known as the Captain's House or the Widow's Walk, was built in the early 1800s by an enterprising young man named Thomas Dalton, who sadly died intestate. The Captain's House sits at the top of a long, low hill on Main Street, overlooking Yarmouth Harbour. The large rectangular structure of one and a half stories was accompanied by a single large flat tower in the Victorian style that was added on in later years. This tower was crowned by a widow's walk, and so gave its name to the imposing manor. For those who don't know, a widow's walk is that wee little iron fence you sometimes see atop a large old sea mansion. It surrounds a small railed observation platform and is custom-made for folks who have a reason for watching the sea.

Back in the 1880s, the house was nearly lost in a brush fire which completely destroyed a neighbouring house and barn. The furniture of the Widow's Walk was hastily removed for fear of losing it, yet the brush fire turned away from the house at the last minute. One eyewitness swore that it was "as if the house had simply refused to burn."

Following a surprising number of sales and transactions, the house eventually fell into the hands of Captain Jacob K. Hatfield. Hatfield was born on June 16, 1823, the eldest of seven sons, all of whom went on to become successful ship masters. Jacob himself was the master of a clipper passenger ship sailing between England and Australia for many years. He was often away from his family for long stretches at a time. Such was the life of any sailor, yet Hatfield wanted to be certain that his wife and children were safe. So he purchased the Widow's Walk and installed his family in their brand-new home.

Jacob Hatfield's wife, one Eleanor Jane Hatfield, called Gramma Jane and eventually Gramma Jake, was a tall and handsome woman, although somewhat overweight with age and the strain of raising a large family mostly on her own.

Her heart was broken at the loss of her second son, who sailed away in his late teens to follow in his father's footsteps. He never returned. Some say he was lost in a Caribbean storm, while others claim that he simply fell in love with the open sea and never returned to Yarmouth.

Whatever the case, there was an empty space in the life of Gramma Jake that none of the good intentions and kind words of her neighbours, friends, and family could ever hope to fill.

She kept her son's bed made, set a place at the table for him, and walked and watched for many long hours upon the high and lonely widow's walk.

Her husband died before her and so added to her grief. Her walking continued. Folks would see her up there, as constant as a lighthouse, with memories as her only companions.

Eventually Gramma Jake passed on. Some say that she fell from the widow's walk, while others simply claim she had died in her sleep.

Since her death, the house has been haunted by the apparition of a tall and stately woman dressed in gray or white, in the fashion of the Victorian age. Others have spotted strange lights dancing upon the iron railing of the widow's walk, like the phenomenon known as St. Elmo's Fire. There are some sailors who claim that these mysterious dancing lights have helped guide them into Yarmouth Harbour on foggy nights.

The woman's figure has been seen standing atop the tall staircase up to the widow's walk, and has even been reported to have kissed the cheeks of two young children as they drifted towards sleep.

As lately as the early 1980s there have been reports of strange lights dancing across the widow's walk and the sound of a ghostly bagpipe lament wailing softly in the night.

More recently, the lower floor of the Captain's House has been occupied by a golf shop and later a tole painting shop, but neither prospered. The house is currently inhabited, but even so most folks in Yarmouth steer clear of the Captain's House.

9

THE IRON BOX AT FRENCH CROSS

MORDEN

I am a writer of horror fiction and a teller of ghost stories. I like nothing better than to put a good old-fashioned scare into people. Still, there are events in this world far scarier than my meagre pen can dream up. One such event was the expulsion of the Acadians.

During the late 1600s a population of about one hundred French families settled in Acadia, which at that time consisted of the territories of northwestern Nova Scotia, New Brunswick, and eastern Quebec, as well as part of modern-day New England.

At the conclusion of the Seven Years' War, a beaten France was forced to sign the 1713 Treaty of Utrecht, ceding Acadia to the British, who decreed that Acadia would now be known as Nova Scotia.

At first the occupation was peaceful. The trouble began in 1754, in the middle of the French and Indian War, when the British government demanded that all Acadians living within the borders of Nova Scotia take an oath of allegiance to the British crown.

When the Acadians refused to sign the oath, the British government decided to deport the remaining Acadians and the expulsion officially began.

Hundreds of Acadian homes and settlements were burned to the ground. Families were torn apart and the Acadians were systematically shipped to new homes on both sides of the ocean. They were dispersed to the thirteen colonies, France, Georgia, England, St. Pierre and Miquelon, and Louisiana, where the refugees formed thriving "Cajun" settlements.

In later years, the government officially apologized to the Acadians, yet the expulsion remains a black mark on the scrolls of Canadian and Maritime history.

I found the roots of this story buried in the pages of a short article I found in the March 18, 1889, Halifax *Herald*. It takes place in a little town called Aylesford, situated midway down the north shore of Nova Scotia's Annapolis Valley.

✠

On the northern shore of Nova Scotia, facing the Bay of Fundy, is a massive and formidable wall of cliffside, a naturally formed defence against the sea and any invader. Unfortunately the cliffside seawall also makes a particularly nasty fence.

Directly across from the town of Aylesford is a break in the seawall that the old folks used to call French Cross. Some say it earned its name because of the large cross the Acadians left behind them as they fled their British expellers, while others believe that the name is meant to simply mark the place where the French crossed the Bay of Fundy. Nowadays this location is better known as the town of Morden, a name that echoes strangely the French word for death: mort.

In 1755, Acadians living in Grand Pré and Canard were forced to surrender to the British army.

Several hundred of them were held prisoner in the confines of the Grand Pré parish church, surrounded by a legion of well-armed British redcoats. In the harbour a small flotilla of British ships were eagerly waiting, ready to bear the surrendered remains of the Acadian population to an as yet unknown destination.

The news flashed down the Gaspereau River, spreading like a plague that touched the heart of every Acadian inhabitant in the region. A meeting was called to decide how the remaining Acadians in the area would deal with the British victory. They were split between flight and surrender. About sixty Acadians headed up the river, keeping away from the roads and the clear waterways for fear of the British.

The journey was a costly one. Their supplies quickly ran out and they were forced to subsist upon a diet of berries, fresh fish, and whatever game they caught. Dysentery broke out among the refugees. They were at the mercy of the elements without benefit of any kind of medical aid.

They hid in the Aylesford hills and began digging a series of graves for the increasing number of their dead that eventually came to be known as the French Cross Burying Grounds, a make-shift graveyard in a barren sandy field near where they camped. The refugees lacked even a clergyman to sanctify the burials.

The Mi'kmaq helped the Acadians as best they could, bringing in the game and medicines they foraged. Thus, the Acadians were supplied with deer and moose, and they were able to forage mussels from the rocks of the shoreline. Partridge and rabbit supplemented their meagre diet. The Mi'kmaq steeped alder leaves to treat fever and stomach ailments and to wrap about festering wounds; boneset, bearberry, and poplar leaves were used to treat colds.

The Acadians continued to hide as the autumn dragged slowly into the winter. The Mi'kmaq kept them fed and informed of the goings on in the outer world. They decided that their best plan of action was to stay at French Cross until the early spring, and then to cross the Bay of Fundy and journey on towards Quebec where the French were still welcome. They erected their winter tents over the graves of their people by a brook that emptied itself down into the waters of the Bay of Fundy, where they remained safely concealed from the English forces. They could watch the sea and chart the course of the English sailing vessels. They waited there until the spring. Throughout the winter the Mi'kmaq had helped the Acadians construct enough canoes to travel safely in. They worked through the winter, peeling the birch trees and laying the bark.

By the spring the Acadians were ready for their escape. They said goodbye to their rudimentary huts and hide tents and the graves of their fallen loved ones. They erected a large wooden cross to watch over the makeshift graveyard, then loaded into the canoes and paddled across the tumultuous spring waters of the Bay of Fundy.

No doubt many looked back and saw that large wooden cross make its silent promise to keep watch over their dead. The Acadians made their way to New Brunswick, and most never bothered trying to travel any further. There were friends and family and farmland aplenty. What more did they need?

In later years the British found the graveyard. Perhaps in the heat of war they might have laid waste to it, but years after the old war had ceased, they simply viewed it as the remains of a sad story. Yet night after night, for years to come, the treasure hunters would make their way into the darkness of the French Cross Burying Grounds. Treasure-dowsers and vagabonds alike would root through the bones and the dirt, hoping to find the remnants of French treasure. It was whispered that before fleeing Acadia, the refugees had buried what treasure they couldn't transport in a large coffin-shaped iron box that was supposed to be buried somewhere in the graveyard.

Again and again, the treasure hunters sought out the fabled French Cross iron box, yet all who searched for it ended up poverty-stricken. Men swore that their picks and shovels and pry bars bent and twisted in the hardened Acadian dirt, and many claimed that they were chased from the burial grounds by a long yellow spirit. Others swore that every time they dug down with shovels, they would strike the iron box, and it would travel through the dirt. No matter what the story, the end result was always the same. The treasure was impossible to find.

There are many guesses as to what this treasure might hold. Most talk of golden coins, rare gems, and other valuable collectibles that a typical Acadian dirt farmer might have tucked beneath his seed corn and plow.

For myself, I think the treasure might have been something far more prosaic — perhaps a cherished French psalter, a chalice and candle sticks, or maybe even a portrait of great-grandpère. Who knows? The treasure may be out there still, ready to be dug. Or perhaps it's just a ghost of a treasure, a fantasy wish that's destined never to be found.

10

†HE PIPER'S POND PIBROCH

WINDSOR

I have been a member of the Halifax Storytellers' Circle for a very long time. I first joined when the group met every month at the Alderney Gate Library in Dartmouth. Back then, it wasn't much to speak of, just a friendly little group of folks who got together to tell tales to whatever audience might show up. We've been to a lot of places since then, telling our tales to whoever cares to listen.

This is a story I heard back in 2004 at the Haliburton House Halloween festival just outside of the little town of Windsor, about sixty-six kilometres northwest of Halifax. The Storytellers' Circle was telling tales in support of the event. We were performing outside in the middle of the woods, in a comfortable open canvas tent. The wind was blowing softly through the autumn leaves, and it was perfect weather for ghost tale telling.

Our host told this tale to two separate tours with the help of a ghostly bagpiper who showed up at the appropriate moment. I didn't get to hear this presentation because I was busy telling my own tales in the tent.

It wasn't until afterwards that our host kindly related the tale to me again.

✠

Thomas Chandler Haliburton was born in Windsor, Hants County, in 1796, and gained fame as an author, a lawyer, a politician, and a judge. He is best known for the creation of his cantankerous tale-telling Yankee peddler, Sam Slick, whose clever quips, "barking up the wrong tree," "quick as a wink," "raining cats and dogs," and "facts are stranger than fiction," are perhaps better known than their author.

In January of 1833, Thomas Haliburton purchased forty acres of land located on Ferry Hill, just overlooking the town of Windsor, Nova Scotia. He took it upon himself to name the estate "Clifton" after his wife's own home in Bristol, England. There he and his wife lived happily in their modest one-and-a-half story home.

Today the house looks very different than it did in Haliburton's time. Successive owners have altered and added to the house, but the memories still remain. Some say that the ghost of old Thomas Haliburton still walks these halls and winds his clocks, but that tale belongs to another story entirely.

There is a pond not far from Haliburton House and there is a tale that the locals have been telling for years.

Long before it was called the "birthplace of hockey," Windsor was known as Pesaquid, a Mi'kmaq term meaning "junction of waters." This name referred to the convergence of the Avon and St. Croix rivers which flow into the Bay of Fundy.

The British blockhouse of Fort Edward was built and fully garrisoned in the mid-1700s in Windsor and it is here that we first pick up our tale.

✠

His name was Jamie Donaldson, and he was a piper in the Highland Regiment. He'd been stationed at Fort Edward for some time, and while he was there he fell madly in love with a miller's daughter. Her true name is unknown but for the sake of this story we'll call her Donnalee Jenkins. Let's make her beautiful, as all great loves are, give her curly hair, the colour of a raven's wing, with eyes as sharp as needles and painted the pale haunting blue of summer forget-me-nots.

Every night while he was supposed to be keeping watch Jamie would meet his lover by the pond. It was a dangerous business, skipping out on his duty, but he was young and reckless and madly in love. Soon, orders came down and Jamie Donaldson's regiment was scheduled to ship out.

"I'll run away with you," Donnalee Jenkins swore.

They made a pact to meet that night by the pond, but as fate would have it, the young piper was caught trying to sneak over the wall. He was fortunate that it was only a sergeant who caught him trying to slip away with a bouquet of incriminating forget-me-nots in his hand, picked from beside the stockade wall; his bagpipes were tucked under the other arm.

"And where do you think you are going?" the sergeant asked. "It's a wee bit late for the picking of wildflowers."

Jamie opened his mouth and closed it, trying to remember how to speak, but the sergeant only smiled.

"Got yourself a wee colleen, do you now?"

Jamie shrugged and sheepishly grinned.

"And are you going off to say goodbye to her one last time before we ship out?"

"That's it," Jamie said. "One last time before we ship out."

The sergeant fixed him with a gaze as sharp as any bayonet.

"And you wouldn't be harbouring any wild notions about running off and deserting your post, now would you?"

"Oh no, sergeant, sir," James said, shaking his head so hard he thought it might fall off. "Nothing of the kind."

The sergeant's face darkened like a storm cloud. "Don't you 'sir' me, boy. I work for a living,"

And then he let slip another smile.

"I'm thinking that this post might be a wee bit overprotected. Perhaps it's best if you take some air while I keep an eye out for hostiles. Mind you, be back before roll call. If the captain catches you out playing tomcat, it'll be both of our heads that roll in the dirt."

So over Jamie went, clambering down the rope he'd slung with the help of the kind-hearted sergeant who lowered his bagpipes down to him. The forget-me-nots were tucked into a pocket in his tunic. Off he went, headed for the pond where Donnalee stood waiting.

Only she hadn't waited. The sergeant's untimely delay had held her lover up just long enough for Donnalee to lose hope.

"He's not coming," she said. "They've caught him and they've hanged him, or he just doesn't love me enough."

She walked six times around the pond as she waited, before finally working up her courage enough to do what she had in mind. She laid her baggage down and picked up a large chunk of granite. Using the ribbons from her hair she tied her skirt up around the rock. Then, holding the dress-bound granite in her arms like the baby that she and James would never have, she leaped into the deep end of the pond.

At the last she thought better of it and kicked for the surface but the rock was far too heavy and bound too tightly. It carried her straight to the bottom. She tried to scream and swallowed dirty pond water and her face turned a colour that nearly matched her forget-me-not eyes.

Not more than five minutes later young Jamie came by the pond.

"Donnalee!" he shouted, but there was nothing but the laughter of an unseen moonlight whippoorwill that answered his call. Jamie circled the pond seven more times until he nearly fell over Donnalee's luggage. Fearing the worst, he knelt and peered down into the water, searching until he saw her staring up at him, her face a pale blue moon of sorrow.

He knelt there and wept until his tears had cried themselves dry. Then he stood up as straight as a trooper on dress parade. He straightened his uniform and scuffed the loose dirt off with his hands.

He scattered the forget-me-nots he'd picked upon the waters of the pond. Then he blew on those bagpipes, a long last haunting pibroch — a lament for the dead. He marched around the pond, playing his last pibroch until the coyotes howled and the hoot owls called back at him. And then he marched straight into the pond, playing the bagpipes right up until the very end.

The forget-me-nots still grow around the Piper's Pond, scattered like a thousand pale blue tears. The legend says that if you run around the pond thirteen times in a counter-clockwise direction, six times for her and seven for him, or once for every full moon in a year, the piper will rise up out of Piper's Pond and begin to play the bagpipes.

Is it true? As Sam Slick was wont to say, "Facts can be stranger than fiction."

11

THE MOOSE ISLAND DEVIL

FIVE ISLANDS

I first heard this tale told over a pitcher of good draught beer at the Lord Nelson Beverage Room in Halifax, a lowly tavern made famous by the fact that it was only the second pub in Halifax to allow women inside its doors. More recently, the pub has served as the first stopping point for many a college student working their way down Spring Garden Road towards the livelier downtown bars. It was fine fishing grounds for a wandering storyteller; the talk was cheap and the beer even cheaper.

The man who told this tale to me gave me nothing more than the barest of bones to work with. Such is a storyteller's lot. A few days worth of digging at the Archives enriched the facts, and I've painted in what details history saw fit to leave out.

✠

Moose Island is the largest of a fistful of islands that jut into the Bay of Fundy at the base of the broad and low Economy Mountain, near Five Islands, Nova Scotia. There's fine hiking here, and in the autumn the turning leaves will tell you stories I could never dream of.

The Mi'kmaq tell us that Glooscap created these islands while throwing stones at the beaver across the bay from the top of Cape Blomidon. The legend goes that the beaver had built a dam between Advocate and Blomidon, causing water to flow into Glooscap's Blomidon home and drown out his medicine garden. Glooscap set a trap to catch the beaver, but the wily animal escaped his device. In a fit of rage Glooscap then threw five great boulders at the beaver, who escaped, but not without a flattened tail.

More practical sources will tell you that the five islands have been christened geometrically for their shape — Diamond, Long, Egg, Pinnacle, and Moose. Moose Island is so named because it looks just like the hump of a big old bull moose rising up from out of the gray waters of the Atlantic.

Upon the granite coastal wall of Moose Island is crudely carved the face of an angry bearded man. Locals call this cliffside Ruff's Ghost after a long dead Irish settler who went by the name of John Ruff.

Back in the mid-1800s Moose Island was the only island of the five that had been settled. John Ruff lived there with his wife Susannah. Together they raised six children – Isaiah, Noah, Andrew, Arthur, Anthony, and Benjamin. Sadly, John was not the best of men. A drinker and an abusive father, he frequently beat his wife and was known in those parts as a bit of a bully. In the late summer of 1842, John and four of his sons were working on Moose Island. Susannah was enjoying a much-needed vacation from John's bullying ways at the settlement of Five Islands. The two oldest sons, Noah and Isaiah, had grown and fled the unhappy family.

On that day in July 1842, the oldest son Andrew rowed the family dory into Five Islands with his father's corpse laid in the stern. John Ruff's head was broken open as if by a bad blow and a single maple leaf was found embedded in the gory wound.

"It was a maple tree did it," Andrew swore. "Father had been drinking and he felled it badly."

As I've said it was a long-known fact that John Ruff was overly fond of the bottle, so no one was surprised to hear this story. The case was quickly dismissed as a simple accidental death, and the town of Five Islands began busily burying the memory of John Ruff and his abusive ways.

But one person could not forget. Young Benjamin Ruff, nine years old at the time of his father's death, was haunted by bitter memories of that day on the island. He was kept awake at night by visions of his father standing with an axe over his bed. For two long years, young Benjamin feared the coming of nightfall and the blind baleful stare of the Atlantic moon. Then, two years from the date of his father's death, young Benjamin felt compelled to make a startling confession to the authorities.

"It was Arthur and Andrew who murdered Father, and Anthony and I saw the whole thing happen."

The two older boys were brought in for questioning, but it was taken to be a bad sign when Arthur Ruff fled the district. The truth came out when young Benjamin told a Supreme Court in Truro of what had happened on the night of his father's death.

"Father had been drinking," young Benjamin said, "and he'd gone to lay down in the barn with my older brother Anthony. He was asleep when Arthur went and got the axe. Arthur stood over Father for a long time, waiting for him to wake up. When he opened his eyes, Arthur brought the axe down on his head."

Benjamin further stated that Arthur and Andrew had dragged their father's corpse out of the barn to the woods, where they prepared a crime scene, felling a heavy maple tree and placing their father's corpse next to it. While Arthur arranged the corpse, Andrew went back to the barn and used a hand adze to hew and gouge out the bloodstains on the floorboards.

"Why did they do this? Why did you say nothing until now?" the prosecuting attorney asked young Benjamin.

"I didn't want my brother to hang. It wasn't any of his fault."

"Whose fault was it?"

Young Benjamin's eyes grew strange and flat and he stared over the courtroom in a cold and distant fashion.

"We saw something strange that night before the killing — a dark figure dancing about the barn," Benjamin said. "I think it was the devil."

The other sons confirmed that there had been many times in the past when this devil had been seen upon the island.

Was it one more lie? The product of a deluded boy's vivid imagination? Or was it perhaps the truth?

"The devil likes it there on the island," Andrew swore. "He whispers in the night. I think it was his idea that Arthur kill father."

"And was it the devil's idea that you hide your father's murder in such a fashion?" the prosecuting attorney sarcastically asked.

"No, of course not," Andrew replied. "We didn't want to see our brother hang. One death in a family is bad enough, don't you think?"

"We saw the devil once before," Benjamin later added. "My sister saw him behind the water barrel when my father was going to kill Mother with his knife, but when Father saw the devil looking at him like a hungry man watching a stew pot steep, he couldn't do it."

Further questioning brought to light the fact that the boys had originally planned to throw their father over a cliff and had gone so far as to practice by throwing a sheep over the cliff. Because the sheep was only crippled by the fall, they decided to find themselves another plan.

Ruff justice, indeed.

The Ruffs' barn had tumbled down in a storm, but officials investigated the wreckage nonetheless. They discovered evidence of a chipped floor and bloodstains between the cracks of the floorboards, but that was a common sight in the days when farmers slaughtered their livestock indoors. The coroner exhumed Ruff's badly decomposed body and ruled that although the wound to the skull could indeed have been caused by a malicious blow with an axe, it could just have easily have been caused by a poorly felled tree. This testimony was further substantiated by townsfolk who allowed that Ruff was a poorly skilled woodsman, a bit of a drunkard with a bad temper to boot. Another witness declared that he'd never believed young Benjamin was of a right mind.

After further questioning, the judge ruled in the accuseds' favour. He decided that the evidence presented by a delusional eleven year old wasn't substantial enough to convict Andrew and Arthur.

The blame was laid at the feet of the earlier magistrate's failure to summon a coroner at the initial time of death. Lack of evidence was the final verdict, and the death of John Ruff, axe blow or not, was deemed accidental.

The Ruffs soon left the island, not even bothering to sell the property. As far as the townsfolk of Five Islands knew, young

Arthur never returned to the area. Yet lights have been seen to this day on Moose Island, strange dancing lights, like a lantern being held by a shaky man, or a ghost.

Is it the devil, or the ghost of John Ruff? Perhaps it is the spirits of his murdering sons, doomed to endlessly repeat their crime. I dare you to spend a night camping on this island to find out the truth.

12

THE WEEPING CAVE OF PARRSBORO

PARRSBORO

This story was told to me by a Saint Mary's University professor of Mi'kmaq descent. He was a bit of a wild man and taught me that a writer shouldn't feel shackled by the chains of conventionality. One of my fondest memories was of him walking into class with a stick of high explosive and placing it on his desk.

"Sometimes," he said to the class, "a writer needs to use dynamite."

Of course, no English students were harmed in the making of this anecdote.

The dynamite was a dud.

I hope you'll find this story isn't.

✠

The shores of Nova Scotia are riddled with caves, the most famous being The

Ovens sea caves of Riverport, Lunenburg County. Every year thousands of tourists make the climb down to view these spectacular rock formations and listen to the waves echoing their long lonely song.

If you happen to travel to Parrsboro, the folk there will be glad to tell you about the mystery of the Maiden's Cave, where the ghost of a young woman weeps and moans to this very day.

You'll find Parrsboro on the northern shore of the Minas Basin. It was named in the year 1784 in honour of Admiral John Parr, who was Governor General of Nova Scotia at the time. Before that Parrsboro was simply known as the Partridge Island settlement. It is reputed to have the world's highest tides and has been celebrated as the home of Glooscap, mighty Mi'kmaq warrior and magician. The area is also well known for the amazing amounts of amethyst and agate that can be found on beaches and cliffsides. Legend has it that while creating the tides, Glooscap scattered his grandmother's jewelry bag on the shores of Parrsboro, thus creating its abundance of natural wealth.

In John Parr's time, the waters of Nova Scotia were home to scores of ruthless pirates and privateers. One such pirate, a Sicilian by the name of Dionaldo, was making a fine living pirating the boats that passed by.

Mention pirates and people will picture sashes, cutlasses, and golden hoop earrings, men shouting "Yo ho!" and swinging from ropes with knives in their teeth, or one-legged sea captains with gaudy parrots perched on their shoulders. That's not how it really was. More often than not, a pirate would simply pull up beside your ship, possibly with two or three ships of his own, and point a cannon at your ship's hull. You would be given the option to surrender, and perhaps become a pirate yourself. If your ship was deemed seaworthy, the pirate would seize it and hoist his own flag, thus increasing his flotilla. Pirating was a business, plain and simple.

Mary Jane Hawkins sailed with her father on trading missions in his ship, the *Red Hawk*. Some swore that a woman on board a ship was simply asking for bad luck, but Mary Jane's father held no such belief. Being both captain and owner of the ship, his word held sway over all the crew's fears.

Yet perhaps the crew had been right in this instance.

The trouble began when Dionaldo's vessel came aside of the *Red Hawk*. The captain would not surrender and so he and the crew were massacred. Mary Jane, however, was saved for other purposes. Knowing what her fate would be, she tried to fling herself overboard, but Dionaldo would have none of that. Had circumstances been different, this tale might have ended a little more abruptly. Possibly Mary Jane might have escaped or drowned herself. Perhaps Mary Jane might have married Dionaldo and lived as a pirate-captain's wife.

At least that was how Dionaldo saw it. You see, Dionaldo was a bit of a romantic. He believed that he could woo this daughter of the sea, and that in time she would certainly fall in love with him. He couldn't fathom the notion of her holding a grudge simply because he'd killed her father and all of her friends. She was just a girl, after all, and as wayward as the restless sea. He was certain her mood would turn, and she would find her way to his bunk. You've got to love an optimist.

For several months he kept her locked in a ship's cabin, feeding her scraps and trying to win her over. He would let her walk the deck every evening, leashed with a stout rope tied at his side. He talked to her, telling her the tales of bravado and adventure that he had lived through. He told her of how in the long nights when he'd stood at the wheel, he'd looked up into the northern skies and seen the colour of her eyes. Our Dionaldo was also a bit of a poet, and a charmer to boot.

"I will give you precious gemstones and make you my bride," he swore.

Yet Mary Jane could not forget the sight of her dying father. At the earliest chance, she stole a dirk and tried to cut Dionaldo's throat. He was too quick, though, and took the knife away from her.

"If you prefer the embrace of the sea to my arms, you shall have your wish," Dionaldo swore.

He would have thrown her overboard, but the sudden intervention of a British man-of-war saved Mary Jane from a watery grave. The pirate ship slipped away and found itself off the coast of Parrsboro, then uninhabited. Dionaldo took the girl ashore and accomplished his terrible revenge. He sealed her in a cave filled with raw amethyst and quartz, with a few salted pollack serving as her meagre provisions.

"You see," Dionaldo howled. "I swore I would give you gemstones, and so I have."

They sealed up the cave with rocks and covered the rocks with underbrush, and left Mary Jane to her lonely doom. Some say she died, some say she was rescued, and some say she is out there still.

There are quartz crystals that can be found in this area that are grown in the shape of smooth teardrops. Some claim they are the last teardrops that Mary Jane wept.

The Mi'kmaq shunned this area because of the cave, and at certain times when the wind is right the folks around Parrsboro claim that you can still hear the ghost of Mary Jane Hawkins weeping over her lonely fate.

13

THE HIDEY HINDER OF DAGGER WOODS

ANTIGONISH

Hip-deep in my research for this collection I came across a mention of a demon that was reputed to haunt the Dagger Woods of Antigonish County.

I couldn't find much more than a brief description of the creature, but it sparked a memory of a story that I'd heard of a Hidey Hinder that followed hikers around in the Cape Breton Woods. I had discovered two perfectly good pieces of two completely different jigsaw puzzles, and I decided they might fit together nicely.

There are an awful lot of stories told about Dagger Woods, just a long forest road about fifteen kilometres east of

Antigonish. You can walk through if you like. By daylight it doesn't seem like much, but nightfall brings another story. Residents will tell you of the strange and awful cries that sound throughout the woods. Others talk of a gray-clad demon wearing a bright red cap who will follow you around. They call it the Hidey Hinder, and it's said that it will sneak up on unwary hikers and follow them on their way.

You'll hear it, sneaking and creeping up on you, just behind your left ear, but try as you might, you can't see it. Turn as fast as you like, and the Hidey Hinder is that much faster. It's worse than trying to catch a mosquito while blindfolded. The Hidey Hinder keeps in your shadow, hiding just behind you, and the only way you can save yourself is to catch a single glimpse of him. That's the hard part. He always moves just that much too fast to be caught.

Some say he's just a fooler, a minor level trickster who is looking for a giggle on you. Others say that he will chase you until you panic and run, and that the bones of those who died of exposure and lie lost in the woods are usually scarred by the long-fanged hunger marks of the Hidey Hinder.

✠

Young Saundra Girard wasn't thinking of anything but the fat August blueberries she would gather in her bucket. She couldn't wait to hear that juicy plump hollow sound that the blueberries would make as she dropped them into her bucket – plunk, plunk, plunk. That was her favourite sound. She loved to hear the sound soften as the bucket slowly filled until at the very end of it when she would have to place each blueberry very delicately, one by one, for fear of over-spilling her bucket.

Sometimes she would take a fruit basket left over from the groceries and fill it with white foam cups. Then she would fill each cup with blueberries, saving the fattest and the best for the very top. Once the cups were filled she would wait by the road for the bus and sell the berries to the hungry passengers for a dollar a cup. Her mother had done this as a child, selling the berries for twenty-five cents a cup, and before that her grandmother had peddled the blueberries for ten cents a cup.

Today's blueberries weren't to be sold, however. Today's blueberries were strictly for baking. Saundra had already decided what she wanted her mother to make with the berries: a great big feed of blueberry muffins. Saundra loved her muffins fresh and hot from the oven, just cooled long enough to handle without a mess. She'd slather them up with butter and eat them until her belly pretty nearly burst.

That's why she was out this far in the woods. She needed to find her berries, and the best ones grew thickest out in Dagger Woods. A lot of kids she knew stayed out of these woods, because folks thought they were haunted. Some people said that a man had died in a knife fight in these woods, and that his ghost still waited with a drawn knife, looking for revenge. Her Uncle Roderick said that there was a demon out here haunting through the shadows and searching for fresh meat.

Saundra wasn't scared. The only thing that scared her was the thought of how close it was to back-to-school time. She wasn't looking forward to having to sit at a desk all day long. The schoolhouse frightened her more than any monster ever could. Just thinking about that big old schoolhouse with its doors hanging open like a dragon's jaws was enough to scare the living daylights out of her.

The woods didn't scare her one bit. She never got lost and even if she did she knew how to find herself again. Her daddy had taught her that trick. "Lost is a surprise that sneaks up on you, just around the very next corner," he always said. "Look for the water. Remember the track of the stream and follow it on back home. A good river or a stream can be just as dependable as a highway."

Saundra had listened. She knew that you had to be careful in the woods, and she always was.

She kept on walking. She was close to where the blueberries grew fattest. This was her secret spot, out here in the pine trees. There'd been a fire ten years back and nothing grew blueberries like burned-over woodland.

She knelt in a patch of berries. The rock she squatted on was a little tippy so she turned it over. A big fat red centipede scuttled out from under, all wet and nasty. She drew her breath in sharply and held it for a half an instant. In that half an instant she heard a branch snap behind her like the wishbone of a chicken.

She turned, half-expecting to see a deer, a rabbit, or at worse a bear. Bears were hungry this time of year, looking for berries to fatten themselves up for hibernation. The cubs would be mostly grown, not needing their momma's protection, so the odds were any bears would be more than happy to leave her alone.

She saw nothing.

And then she heard it again, softly to her left, a dead leaf crushed beneath an unseen pressure — a heavy footstep sounding very close indeed.

She held still, not wanting to disturb whatever it was that had made the noise. She edged her glance backwards, slowly pivoting her head in tiny careful increments — nothing.

And then she heard it, even closer, just behind her left ear, a soft damp giggle.

"Jeremy?"

She whirled around as fast as she could, trying to catch a glimpse of her mischievous older brother.

Still nothing.

"Jeremy if you're trying to scare me it won't work. You know I can hear you."

But that was the point. She was supposed to hear it, supposed to be terrified and to run screaming into the wilderness. Maybe fall down and twist her ankle and lie there starving to death. Perhaps she'd run into a tree or fall off into a rock cut.

She felt its hot breath upon her neck. She shivered, as if she were cold. She remembered a time when she and Jeremy had found a dead dog beside the roadway. The dog had been covered in maggots that had made a soft sound like crackling cellophane. The stink had been terrible.

This thing's breath was worse.

Now she was remembering her father's voice. She was remembering a story he'd told about the Hidey Hinder, how it would creep up and follow hikers through the woods, scaring them into hurting themselves, or panicking and becoming lost. Her father had said that the only way to scare a Hidey Hinder off your trail was to catch a look at it; it couldn't stand the sight of its own reflection in another's eyes.

Saundra felt something move closer to her. She heard a soft, rancid giggle, like someone snickering through a mouthful of bad butter. She jumped, just as fast as she could, whirling about three times fast, stopping at every whirl and trying to catch a look at the Hidey Hinder: nothing, nothing, and still more nothing. She jumped and whirled and jumped and whirled, trying to catch a glance at the elusive beast but all she caught was a really bad case of the dizzies. She nearly tripped and fell.

"You'd like that," she thought. "You'd like that a whole lot, wouldn't you, Mr. Hidey Hinder? You'd like it if I tripped and fell and hurt myself. You'd laugh at me while I lay there and rotted down into something soft enough for your rotten old teeth."

She forced herself to be still. She waited for the world to stop spinning before her eyes. She forced her breath to slow down, and then that thing behind her stuck its slimy tongue against her ear.

Saundra took off running like a sprinter at the sound of the starter's pistol. She crashed straight ahead, twisting and turning and trying to look back over her shoulder to catch a look at the Hidey Hinder.

It was no good. No matter how hard she tried, she caught no more than a fleeting glimpse of its shadow. The shadow looked large, larger than a shadow ought to be. It looked hungry.

She kept running, and in the midst of her panic she heard her father's voice, telling her to run for the stream. She knew it was over one more hill. She could hear the Hidey Hinder close on her heels.

"I just have to stay ahead of it," she thought. "It's not trying to catch me. It's just trying to scare me." It was working. She was scared stiff. Her breath was burning her lungs, and her legs felt like they'd been poured full of sand. "Just a little further," she thought. "Just up over the hill."

There it was: the stream, bubbling and laughing around the rocks, the most beautiful sight she'd ever seen. She ran for it and fell to her knees, scraping one against a stone. She looked down into the water and saw the reflection of the Hidey Hinder, and that was all it took. There was a puff of foul-smelling smoke and that was the end of the Hidey Hinder. She was safe.

Saundra hurried home as fast as she could. She hugged her brother hard, her mother harder, and her father hardest of all.

"So what'd it look like?" they asked, after she'd told them what had happened. "What did the Hidey Hinder look like?"

She wouldn't say, or perhaps she couldn't.

It was a long time before she found the nerve to ever go back into the woods, and when she did, she always carried a pocket mirror, just in case that old Hidey Hinder came sneaking up behind her.

14

THE BLACK DOG OF ANTIGONISH HARBOUR

ANTIGONISH HARBOUR

Legends of eerie black dogs, with names such as Barguest, Shuck, Grim, Black Shag, Trash, Skriker, Padfoot, Ku Sidhee, are scattered throughout Celtic history. These dogs are frequently thought to be forerunners of death. They are seldom found very far from the sea, and some folklorists believe them kin to the man-eating water horse or the selkie seal people.

Originally told in the British Isles, these stories migrated with the British and Scottish settlers, following them all the way to Nova Scotia.

This is one I heard around a campfire. I've added a little to it.

✠

To say that Willis Dougall was a drunkard was a little like calling an ocean deep. Willis used to tell his friends that he'd been born in a drought year with a thirst that ran bone deep. He was, as folks would say, clearly under the care of the bottle, and he'd lost track of the cork a long time ago.

One fine Nova Scotia morning, Willis Dougall set out for the town of Antigonish, accompanied by his brother, Dane. They decided to ride along the sunny reaches of the harbour. They rode up and over and down the steep rugged North River hill through the level stretches around the landing where the ships came in. They paused once by a traveller's cairn to lay a stone for luck. This was an old custom, still practised in other parts of the world. Folks passing by would lay a rock on the cairn, and as you passed by, you would lay one too. Thus luck was shared, for a wanderer's fate is always written in stones. Besides, it was an excellent way to make sure that the path was always cleared of stones.

The two brothers then rode up the long and torturous slope of Mount Cameron, until they finally came to the quiet little town of Antigonish.

There, Dane and Willis parted ways, swearing that they'd meet in the afternoon, once they'd properly fortified themselves for the long ride home. Dane went to the parsonage for a blessing for the road, while Willis headed straight for the local tavern.

Well, a promise easily made is even more easily broken, and by the late afternoon Dane was still waiting impatiently for Willis. Finally, he hunted his brother down in the tavern where young Willis was attempting to drink Antigonish dry. Willis was as sodden and maudlin as a drunkard could be. "I'm no good," he moaned. "You should leave me here in the tavern with the rest of the riff-raff."

But Dane would hear nothing of the sort. "I promised Mother I'd see you safe and home and promises are made to be kept," he said, feeling a little smug about his own high moral standards. After much effort, Dane finally managed to hoist his drunken brother up onto his horse, and he led him off homeward.

The trouble came when they came to the North River Hill traveller's cairn.

"Stop the horse, stop the horse," Willis protested.

"Will you be laying a rock, then?" Dane asked.

"No," Willis said. "I have to make a wee warm rain."

Now the North River Hills are no place to be stopping on the night of a full moon, for the hills were known to be haunted by ghosts and spirits alike. Some claim that there is a doorway to hell hidden somewhere on these hills.

"Don't be peeing on the traveller's rocks!"

"And why not?" Willis retorted. "What else are they good for?"

And so Willis made his wee warm rain upon the traveller's cairn.

As they rode down towards the harbour they felt as if they were being followed. They looked back and saw that a big black dog, long of shank and heavy of head, was trailing them over the hills.

"It's the black dog," Dane swore.

Willis sobered slightly at the sight of this great black hound. He had heard his grandfather tell tales of the black dog that would stand outside your door and warn you of your impending death. The devil's hound, some folks called it.

They tried to drive the hound off by hurling rocks and broken branches, but they had no luck; the beast kept after them.

They rode hard over the hills. Two hours later they'd managed to reach the shelter of Dane's cabin. Dane lit a fire in the fireplace and laid his brother on his very own bed.

"It's come for me," Willis said.

The black dog set up an unholy clamour, baying and banging its paws against the outer door.

"For you or for me or for both of us — it does not matter. I've sworn to protect you, and no hound of hell will cause me to break my word." With that, Dane barred the door and fired a blast from his musket out of the window slit at the black dog, to no avail.

The dog kept watch. All grew silent. After a time, as the darkness of the night increased, the brothers thought they were safe. Then, as if he'd always been sitting there, the black dog stepped out of the shadows of the bedroom.

Stunned, Dane threw an iron poker at the hound, but he might as well have been tossing goose feathers at the beast. The big dog made for the bed. It was Willis he was after.

"I'm done for," Willis moaned.

"Not so long as I draw breath," Dane swore. "A brother is a brother." He ran and grabbed his father's claymore from above the fireplace. A great long sword used by the Scottish highlanders at the battle of Culloden, it made a suitable axe, perfect for cleaving off the heads of your enemies. The hilt was still stained with Dane's grandfather's blood. Since then the sword had been blessed by a saint, a bishop, and a beggar. Dane hoisted it up in both of his hands.

"The Lord is my shepherd," he shouted. "I shall not want."

Dane chased the black dog from the house, shouting the Lord's Prayer and the twenty-third psalm at the top of his lungs, along with a half a dozen salty Highland curses. He chased the dog out into the night and for a long time afterwards, everything was deadly still. Willis cowered in his brother's bed, whispering a prayer over and over to himself.

Later the next day, they found Dane's claymore on the North River Hill, imbedded deep in the dirt directly next to the traveller's cairn.

Dane was never seen again, and Willis died three years later, never touching a drink nor breaking a promise again. He spent his last three years searching the North River Hill, and some say that he died near that cairn, where his spirit walks the night, still searching for the remains of his long-lost brother.

15

THE CAPE NORTH SELKIE

CAPE NORTH

The old folk tell us that when the angels fell from heaven, some fell on the land and some fell upon the sea. Those that fell upon the land became fairies, and those that fell upon the sea became the selkie.

The selkie are a race of seal-people, who live in the ocean as seals, but periodically return to the shore to frolic as humans. Sometimes a selkie will marry a mortal man or woman, and then they can never return to the sea, lest the seal form take and trap them.

I heard this tale of the selkie from an old Cape Breton woman. We were standing on a beach when she told it to me, and even now, as I write these words, I can still recall the screeling of the fishing gulls and the soft-talking hush of the rolling Atlantic waves.

They say that there's a tale for every wave that washes the shores of Cape Breton.

This is one of them.

✠

Angus Lochaber was a poor but proud man who made a living on the shores of Cape North, just a little ways out of the town of Bay St. Lawrence. One morning he was out digging in the tidal flats for bloodworms, the best live bait a man could ever dream of fishing with. At the same time he was gathering a pile of driftwood, good for burning since firewood was hard to come by. It was early in the day and the tide was slipping away. A man had to have his wits about him on the mud flats, though. If he lost track of the time, that tide might catch him, and a wayward current might pull him under. The mud flats were where the land dreamed of the sea, and it was not a particularly safe place to linger.

Angus wasn't worried. He'd worked these lands since he was a boy, and he felt as safe as houses out here on the mud flats. He bent and pried out what looked to be a part of a keel, when he heard the sound of a small child crying.

"It's the sea birds," he told himself. "They're crying out there for fish."

But it wasn't the sea birds.

The sound seemed to be coming from a little nook in the rocks. Angus clambered over the rocks, following the sound, his quest for firewood and worms momentarily forgotten.

The sound got louder, rising and falling, nearly human in its tone. Angus slid down a oblong boulder and finally found what was making the strange cries. It was a small gray seal trapped in a pool by the receding tide and a shifting rock that had pinned it to the shore. The gray seal looked up at Angus and its eyes were soft and brown and full of tears.

"Since when does a seal know how to cry?" Angus wondered aloud.

He bent and put his weight against the rock, prying it off the gray seal's back. He scooped and hoisted the seal up and out of the tide pool, when to his astonishment, the animal reared itself upright and its soft gray pelt slid away. Angus caught it instinctively.

Now, standing before him was the most beautiful woman he could imagine. She was tall and wild and fey with hair tumbling down like auburn waterfalls, tangled with seaweed and bits of deepwater shell. She stared up at him with eyes as gray as the November Atlantic. She was shaking, but somehow Angus knew that she was not afraid.

"You've caught me, man of the land — caught me by the code and the law of the sea. You hold my pelt, and so long as you do, I am yours to command."

Angus looked at his unexpected prize. She was a selkie, he knew that. He had heard the tales of how you could keep a selkie by hiding her pelt, how you could bind them to the land and forbid them the sea.

"Then I must give this back to you," he said, handing her the pelt. "For I cannot hold such a wild, free thing as you. You belong to the sea. I give you back to her."

She stared at him, her eyes as wide as the sky and the sea and all that stretches beyond them.

She took the pelt carefully from his hands, and as her hand brushed his, Angus thought to himself that her touch was even softer than the pelt had been.

"You have done a kind thing today, Angus Lochaber," the sea woman said. "The sea remembers longer than the land can ever forget."

And then she kissed him, just once on the cheek, and it was softer yet than anything Angus had ever dreamed of.

Three years passed, and Angus found himself a wife. Her name was Marjorie and she was a good woman. She was neither beautiful nor enchanting, but she made fine biscuits and listened intently to Angus's talk of the sea and his days.

Three more years passed and Marjorie gave birth to a son, a fine young boy that they named Milton. His hair was thick, even at birth, and there was something in it that reminded Angus of the tossing waves.

"This is a good life," Angus said to his wife. "What more could a man ask for?"

Angus loved his family with the heart of a man who has done without for all of his life. Yet sometimes at night when the wind blew soft and cool from the Atlantic waves, Angus would stand at the door of his shanty and stare into the darkness, dreaming of a long-haired woman with eyes as gray as the November storms.

In three more years Angus and Marjorie were given another child, a girl they named Mairgret, in honour of Marjorie's grandmother. For a long time all was well. Then one fine April morning Marjorie, Milton, and baby Mairgret were down on the beach gathering kelp. They'd been at it all morning, and had lost track of the time. The ocean had stolen up on them, and before they realized it, they were cut off from land.

They took shelter on a small rocky knoll, but Marjorie knew well enough that before too long, the tide would cover that as well.

"Let's pretend it's night time," Marjorie said. "Say your prayers, young Milton. Say your prayers for sleep is near."

"But I don't want to go to sleep, Mother," said Milton.

"We're just pretending," said Marjorie.

The ocean came up, slow and creeping, the waters cold and merciless. Marjorie stood up as tall as she could, holding baby Mairgret in her arms with young Milton balanced high upon her shoulders.

"What fun this is!" Marjorie said, doing her best to keep her fear from the children.

"Momma, I'm scared," said Milton, teetering upon her shoulders.

"No, this is fun," Marjorie said. "Playing in the sea like this."

"Oh look, Momma!" Milton said. "Seals. See them swimming."

Marjorie looked out and sure enough, there they were. Dozens of them, swimming towards her rocky perch. The seals clambered up onto the rock. Marjorie had never seen so many seals so close before.

One great grey seal swam into Marjorie's legs, doing its best to knock her over. She fought the seal just as hard as she could but the other seals joined in. It was difficult trying to keep her balance, while also trying to kick free from the seals' apparent attack.

"What do you want?" Marjorie screamed, as if she expected an answer.

Then her feet slipped on the wet rock, and she felt the water rising up about her. Milton toppled off her shoulders and she reached for him, dropping baby Mairgret.

"Mairgret," she screamed, and then Marjorie was in the water as well.

Marjorie had just enough time to catch one good breath and then she was under. The seals were all around her in the water, moving like sleek dark eels. She felt frightened of them. She'd never known a seal to attack a human, but an animal was an animal.

She tried to keep herself afloat and at the same time retrieve her children. It was an impossible task; the ocean was unforgiving.

She gave up hope and was just about to open her mouth and let herself drown when she felt something moving beneath her. It was three seals, guiding her upward to the surface.

She looked around in utter confusion, not believing her eyes. There was Milton, atop a great bull seal, and baby Mairgret hanging tight-fisted to a grey seal's velvety hide. The seals carried Marjorie and her children back to the shore.

Safely back on land, Marjorie and her children stood before the most beautiful woman that they'd ever seen, with eyes that were wild and gray and hair that tossed behind her like the surf upon the beach.

"You tell your husband that the sea remembers," the sea woman said. "You tell him that one spared to the water is worth three spared to the land."

Her eyes flashed as she spoke, and for a moment Marjorie was uncertain as to whether she saw tenderness, fury, or the soft pang of regret there.

Marjorie and her children returned to Angus and told him of what the seal woman had said. Angus only nodded his head, hugged his wife, and kissed his two children. If there were any tears that fell, he blamed it on the sea mist.

Angus and his family lived for many a year in happiness and contentment, and on the nights when her husband would sometimes walk long hours by the shores of Cape North, Marjorie did her very best to pay it no mind.

When Angus finally died, Marjorie buried him close to the rocks and the waves and the sea that he'd loved so dearly, but she left explicit instructions that she was to be buried close to her parents in the small town churchyard.

To this day the seals still cry and swim about Cape North, mourning the passing of Angus Lochaber.

16

THE SONG OF
THE PIT PONY

SYDNEY

My father was a coal miner. It wasn't the
first job he had, but it was the one he
held the longest. He worked in an open
pit mine just outside of the little town of
Blairmore, Alberta, a little collection of
houses and trailers scattered in the foothills of the Rockies like a heap of forgotten toys.

Dad operated a large dump truck for a
while. I still have a scrapbook photograph
of him leaning his large frame against a
tire nearly as tall as himself. He graduated
from the truck to an even larger steam
shovel. I still remember my grandmother
telling me about how my dad broke a
bone in his foot from falling off his shovel.
In my twelve-year-old mind I wondered
how much of a klutz my dad must have
been to have fallen off a garden spade.

That is, as far as I know, the extent of my coal-mining ancestry, and yet I tell you truly that I can hear the ringing of a coal miner's pickaxe, deep in the caves and tunnels of my race memory. We all feel it, here in Nova Scotia. There's a little coal dust in your every inhalation within our provincial borders.

✠

Men in the coal mines live closely with the shadow of death. You could die beneath a rock fall, or you could bust your guts swinging a pick. You could die of the damp. Death is just another foreman looming over you and there is no telling when he'll tap you on the shoulder and tell you to come with him.

There are very few ghost stories to be found in the mines. The men consider themselves a kind of living ghost, the coal dust nestling in their lungs, the dirt working into their pores, as they climb daily into the grave.

This is a tale of the old days, when men still marched into the mines with pickaxes, shovels, and hand drills slung over their shoulders, and lunch boxes clutched firmly in hand. In those days, coal was trucked out in cars hauled by stout little pit ponies.

The ponies they used were generally Maritime-bred, the only horses tough enough for such extremes. They were usually low-slung and thick of shoulder, chosen specifically for their ability to haul great strings of coal cars through low-roofed tunnels. They were chosen for their temperament; a nasty horse wouldn't get along well with miners and was just as likely to injure one of the labourers.

The mine where the story took place was a dirty place just outside of Sydney, dank and low-ceilinged with a heavy miasma of coal dust in the air and the ground soaked with foul cold black puddles.

The pony in this story was named Pete for the colour of the bog. He was coal black, and the miners hung a pie plate about his neck to reflect their lantern lights. You could hear his hoof beats moving through the mine, a patient clogging like the steady swing of a miner's pick.

Pete was driven by a pit boy by the name of Ethan Brantford. Young Ethan came from a large family, and most of his family worked in the mine. His youngest two brothers picked the slate from the anthracite coal, along with the men too injured to work. His three older brothers worked deeper in the tunnels, two of them picking and hand drilling, and the other performing the "dead work" such as clearing the coal as it was mined and hauling the timber for the shoring of the walls, work that wasn't paid for, but that allowed the older brothers time to bring in the valuable coal. A miner earned more than a labourer.

They all shared the same risks, always waiting for the next "bump." A bump was when the rock shifted, or a pit prop snapped, or a built-up gas pocket ignited. A bump, as harmless as it sounds, usually cost someone his life.

Ethan earned seventy-five cents a day for leading his horse. This was fairly close to a working man's wages back then. He never beat the pony, not once. Beating a horse was generally frowned upon in the mines; a beaten horse tended to become cranky and could not be trusted. Still, even if this were not so, young Ethan and Pete were the best of friends.

To guide the pony through the darkness usually involved a series of spoken commands, but Ethan and Pete worked out a different system. Ethan would sing, and Pete would follow him through the long, winding tunnels. All of the miners got used to the sound of young Ethan walking through the darkness, singing "Barbara Allen": "T'was in the merry month of May, when all the buds were swelling, sweet William on his death bed lay, for love of Barbara Allen."

For three long and dark years, Pete and Ethan worked in a comfortable harmony. Then, one cold September morning as Pete was hauling his load of an even dozen coal cars, the pony stopped short dead in his tracks.

"What's wrong, boy?" Ethan asked.

There seemed to be nothing physically wrong with Pete. The little pony just stood there in the darkness of the mine, shivering softly. Ethan tried to coax him forward.

"Come on Pete. You can do this. I'll give you a carrot."

Not even the promise of a carrot would make the pony move. At a loss for what to do, Ethan tried singing to the pony.

"T'was in the merry month of May, when all the buds were swelling, sweet William on his death bed lay, for love of Barbara Allen."

It was no good — Pete would not budge. The inevitable traffic jam resulted as another load of coal cars rolled up behind Pete and Ethan. The pony and the boy were in the way of the others; the coal needed to get through. The miners had to meet their quota or else go a day without pay.

"Get in front and get ready to lead," said one of the miners. "I'll make him move."

Ethan didn't argue. He was thirteen, and boys of thirteen learned to take orders back then.

The miner uncoiled a bit of rope, looping it double.

"Pony," the miner said. "We'll make quota today, and you've got to MOVE!"

He swung the rope hard against the pony's side, and little Pete jumped forward. He hadn't gone three more paces when the mine shook and a great load of timber and rock came crashing down on Ethan and Pete, killing them both. Those who witnessed the rock fall swore that the pony had sensed the deadly disaster before a single stone had slid.

The miners took the rest of the day off. It was always bad luck to keep working when someone had died in the mine. Sunday was the Sabbath, and there was no work then, but by Monday the mess was cleaned up, and they were ready to go back to work. They shouldered their pickaxes and clambered back down into the mine, talking softly for fear of rousing the dead.

When they reached the site of the accident, they saw a peat-black pony, dragging twelve heavily laden coal cars behind it. The wheels ground against the iron rails and the pony's hooves clopped like a hammer banging nails into a coffin. In the cloying darkness of the tunnel they heard a soft voice singing, "T'was in the merry month of May, when all the buds were swelling..."

As the pony reached them, the ghostly vision faded away, wagon and all. But this was not an isolated incident. Over the next year, whenever a miner crossed this spot, he would hear the horse's hooves clattering against the soft rock, and the soft eerie keening of the boy's last song.

The miners eventually got used to the ghost of the boy and his pony clattering by them in the darkness. Money and need are hard masters, and the fear of hunger can override even the fear of ghosts.

Eventually that tunnel was mined out and sealed off, yet the miners swore in the years to come that they could hear the sound of the horse's hooves clattering somewhere behind the darkness of the rock. Besides the hoof beats, there were those who swore they heard the haunting sound of young Ethan singing softly through every tunnel they passed through, "T'was in the merry month of May, when all the buds were swelling, sweet William on his death bed lay, for love of Barbara Allen."

17

Blood in the Water, Blood on the Sand

SABLE ISLAND

This is a tale that has been told many times and in many ways by such writers and storytellers as Thomas Haliburton, Helen Creighton, and Edith Mosher, among others. The dates attributed to the shipwreck in question have shifted as often as the sands of Sable Island.

So file this tale under "Traditional." It's a tale that has been told so many times that I reckon it's grown straight true.

✠

Sable Island isn't much to look at on the map — just a little strip of sand laid out in the ocean like a curl of bacon in the frying pan. There are some ponies that you've no doubt seen pictures of and a few houses, blown through by the tireless Atlantic winds. No one lives on the island now except for some members of the Coast Guard, a handful of meteorologists, and perhaps a ghost or two.

The island lies there like a fishhook in the water, just waiting for an unwary nibble. Its name, Sable, means sand in French, for a very good reason. Quite simply Sable Island is the world's largest water-bound sand dune, composed entirely of a peculiarly iron-stained quartz and raw red garnet, barely twenty miles long and a mile across. Sailors call it a trap and a snare because of the underwater sandbars that stretch out, like the arms of an octopus, sixteen to twenty miles in either direction of the island's extremities. Between these sandbars lies an unchartable obstacle course of deeps and shoals. The island itself is made entirely of sand, and changes shape as the years go by. The maps must be drawn and redrawn. Two lighthouses, one at each end of the island and built by the Canadian government, have been moved and moved again due to the shifting sands.

The island itself is a kind of shape-shifting ghost; fishermen fear it and sailors avoid it, because the waters about Sable Island seethe with ghosts. Nearly 150 ships have grounded upon the shoals, broken upon the rocks, and sank beneath the churning Atlantic waters surrounding this little stretch of sand.

In the late eighteenth century, the waters of Sable Island claimed a two-masted brigantine by the name of *Frances.* Yet the waters and the rocks were not the only ones that were to blame for the shipwreck. No sir, they had help.

In those days, men known as wreckers made a living salvaging whatever washed ashore. When the pickings were slim and the weather too calm to wreck many ships, there were always a few unscrupulous men who would lay false signal fires, remove warning buoys, and stuff shoal-bells with cotton, thus luring unwary ships to their doom.

It was the wreckers who brought about the end of the *Frances*, luring her to her doom with the aid of several lanterns. Aboard her were a Doctor Copeland, the medical surgeon of the seventh Prince's Regiment, his wife and their two children, fourteen other passengers, and a crew of nineteen men.

Mrs. Copeland was a young woman, younger than her husband by a good six years, and was to all accounts a most beautiful woman with long flowing hair the colour of sunburned straw. She was wearing her wedding ring, a family heirloom of solid silver surmounted by a large red ruby. Those who saw the ring close up described it as an eerie thing, the colour of welling blood.

Frances went down with all hands, and the wreckers found easy pickings, scavenging the supplies and furniture that washed ashore. Amongst the jetsam on the beach, the lead wrecker found the body of Mrs. Copeland. Her face was as pale as candle wax, her skin bloated by long hours in the salt water. Her hair was loosened and snarled by the tide's angry fingers, and her clothes had been nearly torn from her, but the ring was still there. Its beauty caught the wrecker's eye.

He knelt in the surf, heedless of the waves. He caught at the ring and tried to work it from her hand. The ring wouldn't budge; her fingers were swollen from the cold and the long immersion. Stealing a glance to his left and right, making certain no one watched, the old wrecker snapped open his case knife and severed Mrs. Copeland's ring finger.

The instant he cut the finger off, her eyes flew wide open like rudely-snapped window blinds. She opened her mouth to scream, and in panic he held her under the water. She struggled, splashing his face with the blood from her mutilated hand. The wrecker grimly held her under, cutting her throat with the edge of his case knife. In a few short moments, she was dead.

The wrecker stood up, still holding his case knife and the dead woman's finger. He worked the ring off and cast the finger into the tide. He pushed her body out a little ways into the water, saying a prayer to Father Neptune in hopes that the current would catch her and hide his dirty work.

In fear he fled to Halifax, where he sold the ring to a watchmaker of dubious ethics. He used the money to purchase a room and a bottle, and that night he opened his throat with the very case knife he'd used to cut Mrs. Copeland's fair white neck.

Some say it was guilt, and some say that it happened in a fight over the spoils of his crime, while others claim the wrecker was visited that night by the ghost of Mrs. Copeland, who stood over his bedside pointing an accusatory finger stub.

I cannot say for sure, but I do know this. On lonely summer nights when the mist hugs the shores of Sable Island closer than a widow's veil, sailors say that a gray lady may be seen walking through the mists, pointing with the stub of her missing finger. And to this day as the sun slowly sinks, the waters and the sand of Sable Island are still stained a deep and lingering red.

18

THE PHANTOM OARSMAN OF SABLE ISLAND

SABLE ISLAND

As sure as the sunshine follows the rain, one thing will always follow another. In my last tale I told you about Mrs. Copeland's ruby ring and the unfortunate state of her ghostly finger. That tale leads surely to this second Sable Island tale.

✠

Following the wreck of Mrs. Copeland's ship, the *Frances*, the government decided that it would be wise to place a couple of lighthouses upon the hook ends of Sable Island. These lighthouses have been moved, four times since, due to the island's constantly shifting shoreline.

Along with the lighthouses, the government stationed a lifesaving crew of an even dozen men. Twelve souls, and one stout dory.

Some said that twelve men were all who were needed to haul a good-sized dory. It really wasn't that complicated a trick. One man would stand in the bow with a heavy brass sea lantern; he was the boat's set of headlights. A second man would squat in the back, leaning on the rudder; he was the steering wheel. Ten strong lads would haul on the oars, playing the role of the world's very first ten-cylinder search and rescue vehicle.

These twelve men kept watch night and day for any sign of ships in trouble. In stormy weather, and it was stormy more days than not around Sable Island, they'd sit astride their stocky little Sable Island ponies, wrapped in oilskins and gum rubbers, peering into the darkness for any sign of trouble.

They'd keep shifts, some men resting while the others kept watch, so that the dangerous shoals around the ill-fated island were watched over every minute of the day, a necessity in the days before radios and radar. A ship would happen along when it happened along, and the lifesaving crew always needed to be ready for action.

Every four months a second crew would arrive from the mainland, and the first crew would return home: four months on and four months off, that was their shift.

This is the tale of one such crew, during one such four-month-long shift.

The story began on a moonless November evening when the waves were tossing and kicking about Sable Island like a herd of angry horses. The watchman clenched his knees, hanging tightly to his little pony, squinting out to sea, but he couldn't see anything. His ears strained, listening for the grinding of a hull running aground, for the crack of timber breaking free.

I could tell you where he was standing on the shoreline, but what difference would that make? The shores of Sable Island changed with every year. That is why you so rarely see a reliable map of the island; it simply refuses to sit still long enough to be mapped.

And then the watchman saw it. A ship, foundering upon the rocks, caught in the current and the wind, sure to be sunk. He rode full out for the main lodge, and the lifesaving crew ran for the dory.

It's hard work putting a dory out into storm-tossed waters. The currents of the Atlantic tie a knot around the island that unravels any plan.

The crew pushed and hauled hard and the waves kicked them back shorewards as fast as they hauled oar. Sometimes they'd get launched, and sometimes not. Many a time the crew sat shore-bound, the conditions too heavy to launch the dory.

They had to wait until the blow had its temper and was done with, listening for the wails of the drowning carried in on the Atlantic wind. Even when the wind was blowing too hard to hear the screams of the dying, the rescue crew could hear them deep in the pits of their communal conscience.

They hauled the dory out into the waves, standing hip deep in the water with the waves and the wind slashing at them like long wet knives. Finally they were afloat. They rowed out towards the shoal-bound ship, one man in front holding the big brass sea lantern, one fellow in back leaning on the rudder, and ten stout men hauling on the oars. As they approached the shoal, a great wave hooked up and out and dragged the lead oarsman straight into the storm-tossed waves. Down he went in his oilskin jacket and gum rubber boots, three sweaters, and a suit of union long johns. He sank like a dropped anchor and drowned. When you fall into water that cold and deep, there is nothing that can be done; each man knew that. They rowed on, without looking back. They'd lost a friend and a good man, but they had a ship to save.

They rowed out as fast as they could, moving slower now with one less man at the oars. They lost some time correcting their course, as the odd number of rowers kept veering the dory sideways. By the time they'd arrived at the wreck, nearly half of the crew had drowned or perished from the cold.

They shot a line out to the wreckage with a breeches buoy attached: a life preserver with a pair of hip waders sewed in tight. They rowed the survivors to the shore, and saw them safe into the shelters built upon the island for just this purpose. Now, it was time to fetch in the dead.

They'd haul in as many of the dead as they could; later they would comb the beach for the ones who'd washed ashore, sometimes days afterwards. They would sew the dead in a tattered sailcloth shroud, and leave them on the shoreline to be picked up later, by the supply steamer. The sand was too unstable for graves, so the steamer tipped the remains into the open sea. Until the vessel arrived it was the duty of the lifesaving crew to stand watch over the bodies, shooing away hungry gulls and eager crabs.

A couple of weeks after the wreck, there came another ship in trouble. The dory crew rowed out, still short-handed. The survivors of the last wreck had already been picked up by the steamer and taken to the mainland. They rowed out in somewhat calmer water, and as they came to that patch of wild shoals, the lantern man saw a white shape moving in the water.

"It's ice," the lantern man yelled out. "Watch out!"

Only it wasn't ice; it was a body, swimming towards them, the body of their drowned comrade. He swam up to the dory and climbed on board, sat in his usual seat, and began to row. He was a Nova Scotian, and there was no way on God's green earth that he was about to give up on a job half done.

He wasn't pretty to look at. His flesh was soft and bleached from the time spent in the water. There was a little crab clawing through his beard and long sea worms crawling about his body. You could see clear through to his bones in a few spots, but by god, he could row.

The dory crew were astounded by this sight, but being practical fellows they decided there was nothing to do but to keep on rowing. Besides, they weren't about to let a dead fellow outdo them in seamanship.

They made the sinking ship in easy time and rescued all on board. A few of the survivors of the wrecked ship started at the sight of the grisly rower, but the majority of them knew enough of the ways of the sea not to question her work. They looked the other way, or pretended they did not notice. They were mostly just grateful for being pulled from their sinking ship. To them the phantom oarsman was just another sailor in dirty yellow oilskins and a pair of fat black rubber boots.

As the dory crossed over the wild patch of water, the phantom oarsman stood up, tipped his cap like he was saying goodbye and stepped out into the wind-tossed waves and sank beneath the Atlantic.

"His work is done," one oarsman said. "He's gone back to his briny bedroom." But these were hasty words spoken too quickly.

There were two more ships in trouble over that four-month stretch. Both times the phantom oarsman reported for duty, swimming up and clambering into the dory, pulling like mad on the oars, and then finally tipping his hat in a sign of respect right before sinking like a wishing well stone.

Yet time is a river that must always flow forward, and there came a day when the four months of the shift was finished, and the steamer came, bringing along a fresh new crew.

The old crew debated for half of the night before the steamer arrived on whether or not they should tell anyone what they had seen. Word had doubtlessly already escaped from the survivors who had noticed the phantom oarsman. In the end, they decided it best not to tell anyone. If word got out that they'd been seeing a dead man at their dory oars, they might be locked away as lunatics.

"Better not to stir that pot," they decided. "Let her lay and settle."

For a few weeks all was calm with the new crew. They kept their watches, and ran dry-run practices on the shore. Yet things are never quiet on Sable Island for very long. After those few weeks had passed, there came a storm and another ship was in trouble.

The new crew rowed their dory on out across the waves, and as they came to that wild stretch of water, up came the phantom oarsman. He swam straight up to the dory. The men didn't know what to make of him. He looked up into that boat, and saw somebody strange sitting right where he'd always sat.

I cannot tell you if he felt sad or relieved. He just tipped his hat like he was saying goodbye and sank like a stone.

They say he's still out there, to this very day. When the weather is rough and the waters run wild around Sable Island, you might see him swimming through the waves, looking for someone to save, or perhaps someone to save him.

19

THE SALT MAN OF ISAAC'S HARBOUR

ISAAC'S HARBOUR

The town of Isaac's Harbour, Guysborough County, was originally home to a band of Mi'kmaq. Later, a man named Isaac Webb moved his family in. The town was named after him, and if you look closely enough on the map you will find a tiny inlet that is known as Webb's Cove.

The last surviving descendant of this family of original settlers was Henry Webb. He died in 1935 and was buried in the little cemetery at Red Head at the extreme southernmost end of Goldboro. The only standing marker in the entire cemetery belongs to Henry Webb. There were other markers and older graves, but most of these have been washed away with the erosion of the hillside, which faces the sea.

The people of the tiny village of Isaac's Harbour will tell you this tale of a true old salt and his own special kind of burial, if you ask them nicely enough.

✠

John MacNeil was dying. It was his last voyage home from trading in the Caribbean; he was dying of a tropical fever and was afraid of being buried away from home — not for himself, you understand, but for his wife, who would worry about where he lay.

"Don't bury me in the sea," he begged the captain. "For my bones will know no rest and my widow will weep out an ocean over my empty grave."

The captain was a good and honest man who'd known MacNeil most of his life. He hated to break faith with a sailor and a friend.

"I'll do what I can," he promised.

MacNeil passed on that night, but not before wringing one more promise from the captain, who swore on his father's good name that he'd see MacNeil's body laid to rest in the Isaac's Harbour Cemetery.

"In a day's time those old bones will reek higher than three-day-old lobster bait," the first mate prophesied. "That Carib wind isn't blowing up no cooling ice storm, that's for sure. The heat will cook his flesh just ripe."

"We've got an ample cargo of salt, don't we?"

"Aye, for the cod."

"Well, if it's good enough to cure codfish, it's good enough for an Isaac's Harbour boy like John MacNeil, isn't it?"

In those days you either iced your fish down or salted them up, and when you were fishing in Caribbean waters, salt was the only thing that would keep the fish from rotting.

So they decided to lay MacNeil's remains down in the salt. It was grisly work, but fishermen are hardy men. They dug a trench in the salt heap, and laid the body of John MacNeil into it, covering it up with the salt. One bold sailor marked MacNeil's grave with a makeshift wooden cross, but a cross was considered bad luck that would invite a sinking, so the captain made him take it down.

"You see those masts?" the captain asked, pointing up at the mastwork. "That's the only cross a sailor will ever need."

They marked the temporary grave with a hand-painted board that read "Here Lie The Bones Of John MacNeil."

The salt did the trick, and when they arrived home they unshipped his body and carried it on a plank to the Pioneer Cemetery in Isaac's Harbour, where it was buried under the eyes of a holy man and MacNeil's friends and his neighbours. The widow wept long and hard, and she was seen wandering the graveyard at night, barefoot and in her nightclothes, as if in a trance.

Eventually the town decided that in the interest of her safety, it would be proper to bury his body on his own property. They dug up John MacNeil's body one more time and shipped it by wagon under a heavy tarp and an escort of salt flies to the grounds of MacNeil's own home. They buried him there on his own land where his widow could mourn him in peace and not annoy the townsfolk.

Years later the poor woman passed away from long, hard winters of grief. Her family came for her body and buried her in their own graveyard. Another family now owns the MacNeil property, but the salt man still lies buried in his own dirt, and MacNeil's great-grandchildren eventually restored the grave and marked it with a solid brass plaque.

It is said that on certain nights, the folks of the town have seen a woman's figure walking near MacNeil's grave. As it blows over that uneasy grave, the wind sounds like a weeping woman, and on certain nights when the moon hangs high over the fields of Isaac's Harbour, you can hear the ocean calling for its long-lost salt.

20

BIG TONY AND THE MOOSE

MUSHABOOM

I tell my stories through the Writers in the Schools program, with the help of the Writers' Federation of Nova Scotia. Early in my storytelling career I was asked to tell my tales at a school in Shelburne. Being younger and more foolish than I am today, I hitchhiked down from Halifax the night before, and spent a night at a quiet little bed and breakfast where the squirrels were happy to drop acorns on the tin roof all night long. The next day I entertained a half a dozen classes with my storytelling and writing workshops, then set out, determined to hitch home. It was October, however, and it quickly grew dark. I walked for a very long way through the darkness of the highway, in a light tweed jacket and steadily chilling weather. The wildlife entertained me: a deer came out to stare at the fool on the road, and a porcupine snuffled out for a chew on a birch tree. A screech owl shrieked and nearly frightened me to death.

Finally, a kind gentleman stopped and drove me the rest of the way to Halifax. He asked me what I did for a living, and when I told him I was a storyteller, he insisted on telling me this story. I've been telling it ever since.

I knew there had to be some reason I was out there on that road at such a wild time of night.

✠

Just out of the town of Mushaboom, Nova Scotia, there's a soft swampy area that has been known as the haunted bog for as long as the old people can remember.

In the early nineteenth century, a Mi'kmaq the white folk called Big Tony made a living from his hunting, selling the game he caught to the townsfolk. Whatever was leftover, he would eat himself. He made a good enough living for a man of simple needs. Big Tony earned the name because of his height. There wasn't a doorsill in town that he couldn't dust just by walking straight on through. He was strong too; he could pick up a good-sized deer on his shoulders and walk with it. One hunter even swore he'd seen Big Tony walking home through the woods one night with a full-grown moose slung across his shoulders like a baby goat.

Big Tony had an amazing knack for finding game. He'd hunt rabbit and fox and deer, but more than anything else, Big Tony loved to hunt moose. Some say it was the only animal in the woods big enough to feed a man of Tony's size. Others swore he liked to hunt moose because they were a challenge to find.

The real reason Big Tony hunted moose was because they were his totem. He had a bond with the big animals, and they allowed him to hunt his share. Some swore that he spoke their tongue.

Big Tony never lacked for meat, and he made good money selling the surplus to the local market, and those who could afford to hire him swore by his tracking skills. So when three well-to-do Englishmen came to town and asked for Tony, it came as no surprise to anyone.

The Englishmen were looking for moose and would pay a proper guide to take them hunting, providing he guaranteed them a moose. Everyone they spoke to had referred them to Big Tony. So a deal was struck for an honest price, sales tax not having been invented yet.

"Tomorrow," Big Tony said. "You come tomorrow and we will hunt the moose."

Tomorrow came and the Englishmen slept in and arrived late. This was not a good beginning for a moose hunt. To make matters worse, they had brought along several bottles of whiskey.

"Leave the bottles at home," Big Tony said. "Whiskey and gunpowder have never been known to shoot straight."

They laughed at Big Tony's protest. "We are paying you money," they said. "You work for us; you are not our mother. We will do whatever we want to."

Big Tony saw that there was no arguing with the Englishmen, so he went back to his hunting as if they were not there. He was determined to see the job through. He did his best to ignore them, working his way deeper into the soft bog where the moose were usually found.

He moved quietly for such a big man, as soft-footed as the shadow of a cloud, stepping lightly through the dry pine needles and never touching a single broken branch. The Englishmen, however, crashed through the woods — crack, crack, crack — singing and drinking and laughing too loudly at their own bad jokes. Big Tony wondered if they would ever be quiet. You could not expect to find a moose in such a racket, unless you found a deaf one.

The hunting party stalked through the bog all day long, Big Tony tracking as carefully as he could, and the Englishmen making more and more of a racket. Finally, Big Tony had had enough of their foolishness. He turned on them and said, "We have hunted enough today. You are making too much noise and frightening the game. You should pay me now, and we'll go home, get some sleep, and maybe come out tomorrow — without the whiskey."

Big Tony was trying his best to be reasonable. He wanted to believe that the city men didn't know how to hunt, but could be shown how. The Englishmen didn't like the sound of that idea. They got angry, and said they would not pay Big Tony a single red cent.

"Ha," said one of them. "Not a red cent for a red man. That's funny."

Big Tony didn't think that was funny, not one bit. The Englishmen were drunk and angry. They said they weren't going to pay Big Tony. Why should they? He hadn't found them a moose, so why did he think he deserved anything?

An argument is like a little fire. If you aren't careful, it can turn into a blaze; that is just what happened. One of the Englishmen pointed a gun at Big Tony, figuring that was all he needed to end the argument.

It was a big mistake. Big Tony finally lost his temper. As quick as a striking snake, he reached his big hands out and snapped their necks, one after the other — crack, crack, crack!

When he saw what he had done, he felt badly. He hadn't wanted to kill the Englishmen, but what could he do?

He walked into the woods, tired from the day's hunt. Before too long he fell asleep. When he awoke, he was surrounded by white men carrying guns. The townsfolk had tracked him down.

Now in those less enlightened days, if a Mi'kmaq killed a white man, there was very little said about trial or jury. Big Tony tried to explain, but it did little good. A lot of folks hadn't trusted him in the first place. A native man making money? Something certainly had to be wrong.

They marched him out into the swamp, to the biggest jack pine they could find. Then they threw a rope over a high branch, noosed the other end about Big Tony's throat, and hauled the big man up.

It was hard work: Tony was a big man, well over fifteen stone. They'd hoisted him up nearly five feet when — CRACK! — the pine branch broke.

"He is too heavy," one townsman said. "Better drop him from a horse."

"And who is going to risk a horse in this bog? You?"

Big Tony staggered to his feet, shaking his head like a winded animal.

"You are not going to hang Big Tony today," he croaked.

They tried again, slinging the rope up over a higher branch, one that seemed a little sturdier.

They hauled him up again. CRACK! The second branch broke. Big Tony dropped like a hay bale from a toppled wagon. He shook his head again.

"You are not going to hang Big Tony today."

The townsmen were determined. They hauled Big Tony up one more time, using the fork of the trunk instead of a branch.

"Let the red devil break that," one man said.

So up Big Tony went, one more time.

CRACK! Big Tony's neck snapped like a rotted poplar branch. "That'll teach a red man to kill a white," one man said. They let his carcass hang there until the next day.

The next day they returned to the swamp. They had decided to give Big Tony a proper Christian burial.

When they arrived at the heart of the swamp, by the tall jack pine, Big Tony was nowhere to be seen. In his place, hanging by the long hemp rope, was a great red moose.

No one had ever seen a moose that colour before; no one had ever seen a moose that large.

The moose was dead, its neck twisted at an unnatural angle, a clear sign of a rope-broken neck.

After drawing straws, one man cut the rope. As soon as the great moose touched the ground, it stood up on its four legs and walked into the swamp.

Since then folks tend to stay as far away from the haunted swamp as they can. It's a bad place to go hunting, and a worse place to be caught at night; if you're alone in the swamp at night, you're apt to hear a sound — crack, crack, crack — Big Tony, coming after you.

21

THE YONDERSTONE OF WITTENBURG CEMETERY

WITTENBURG

The art of telling tales is a little like that old-fashioned game of telephone. You know the one, where the first person writes down a one-sentence story and then whispers it to another person in the room, who whispers it to a third, until the last person in the party retells the sentence out loud to see how much has been lost or gained in the translation.

This is a tale that was told to me by my wife, Belinda. She heard it from her sister Barb, who says they've been telling this tale a hundred different ways up around Wittenburg, Nova Scotia.

This is how I like to tell it. If you'd like you can tell it to someone else the best way you know how. I won't be insulted if you should happen to misquote me; I'll just blame it on a bad connection.

✠

Tamsen was a wandering child. Anywhere she wasn't supposed to be was where you'd likely find her. And finding her was often the greatest problem. Every time her mother or father called her, Tamsen decided it was a fine time for hide-and-go-seek.

"You can't find me," she'd call. "You can't find me."

She was right about that, for Tamsen was the best of hiders. She could hide in a shadow, behind a root, or under the mossy edge of a rock. She could hide in places you would never think to look.

"A yonder-girl," her grandfather called her. "That Tamsen is a yonder-girl. Wherever you look for her, she's gone yonder."

It was true. Tamsen always wondered what was behind each tree, where each road led, and what lay over the distant ridge of the Wittenburg Hills. Tamsen would play tag with the clouds, chasing them through the fields, trying to catch them. She jumped for birds and whistled for squirrels and hunted after the river endlessly.

"That girl is up to no good," her mother said, shaking her head sadly.

But her father, who had been a long-distance trucker and had worked the railroad line, understood the secrets that were hiding in Tamsen's heart. She was a yonder-girl and dreamed of being somewhere else.

Then one bright November morning, Tamsen wandered too far away.

November is a tricksy month. A day will start out as bright as springtime, but by the afternoon the chill will snap the air and you'll see your breath painting pictures on the wind.

Tamsen set out early that day trying to track the sun. She figured if she followed it far enough, she'd find out where it went down to bed.

Only the sun was faster, and when suppertime came and Tamsen hadn't shown up, the townsfolk went out to look for her.

They wandered the hills of Wittenburg, hunting far and wide for the little girl. They carried lanterns as the night fell on, calling for her, turning over rocks, poking through shadows, and nosing beneath whatever tumble-down log they could find. Caves and nooks and crannies were turned out and over.

Some swore they heard her calling in the distance. "You can't find me, you can't find me." Others claimed they saw her flitting through the darkness, as elusive as the will-o'-the-wisp.

Those who heard her couldn't find her, and those who saw her couldn't catch her.

They searched for three whole days and on the evening of the fourth, they gave the search up as hopeless as an early frost set in.

Not all of them gave up: Tamsen's father continued to search the Wittenburg Hills night and day, carrying a lantern and calling out "Tamsen! Tamsen!" until his voice was hoarse. He searched for weeks, only coming home once in a while to eat.

Then one night he wandered off in his hopeless search and never returned.

They buried a small white casket in the Wittenburg graveyard, under a small, round, white marble stone with a picture of a lamb engraved upon it. The casket was empty, of course, but Nova Scotia folk, living as close to the ocean as they do, have long grown used to the notion of burying an empty casket.

Later that week, when Tamsen's mother went out to the graveyard, the stone was gone. At first she thought that her grief-stricken mind was deceiving her. She brought the sexton out and he looked at his graveyard map; indeed, Tamsen's round stone wasn't where it was supposed to be.

They searched the graveyard until they found the missing stone three sections over, in the sheltered lee of a leaning gray willow.

"Teenagers," the sexton grumbled. "Pranks and horseplay. No telling what they'll be up to next. I'll move the stone back to where it belongs."

"No," Tamsen's mother said. "She's buried here. I can feel it."

Now the sexton had dealt with many a grief-stricken parent before this. He spoke to her as gently as he could, letting his words fall down around her as softly as the gentle autumn leaves.

"You have to let her go," he said. "Your daughter's dead and buried and it's time for you to move on. I'll dig the stone up and move it back to where it belongs.

Tamsen's mother would have none of that. She snatched the sexton's spade away from him and hefted it like an axe.

"If you don't let me dig up my daughter, then I'll stave your head in with this little rusty spade and you can dig one more grave for yourself."

The sexton didn't pause to see if she would make good on her threat; he stepped back and let her dig her grief out. The distraught mother set to digging. Once or twice the sexton made as if to help her, but she spurned his help, snarling at him like an angry mother wolf. Within twenty minutes she'd dug down far enough to come to her daughter's coffin, the small, white, painted box that they'd buried three lots over.

Tamsen's mother stared up at the sexton, dirt on her face and hands. The sexton could only shake his head in bewilderment. This went far beyond any mere prank. The entire grave had up and moved overnight.

"Shall I dig her up and place her back where she belongs?" he asked.

Tamsen's mother shook her head.

"N sense in that. She'll only get to wandering whenever the d strikes her. She's her father's daughter." She looked up wards the far-off hills. "Perhaps she's even looking for him."

So they let Tamsen lie, but she didn't stay put for long, and she hasn't yet.

The people of Wittenburg still talk about the wandering gravestone that moves from place to place and is never where you expect it to be. They'll tell you how people have sat up nights watching it, and sometime during the night between a blink and a nod the tombstone will move. They'll tell you that some days you can't even find it. You might think you see it, that small round white marble stone, and yet as you get closer, it seems to move or change shape or just fade away.

There's some that'll tell you about the phantom light that's seen wandering the bogs and woodlands about the Wittenburg Hills, the ghost of Tamsen's father, still wandering in search of his daughter. But none of them dare speak of the sounds you hear in the Wittenburg graveyard when the November wind is whispering soft and low through the fallen autumn leaves: the high-pitched giggle of a wandering girl and her soft, haunting call, "You can't find me; you can't find me."

---

an was gone.

at the voice calling me; it was the young
er, bustling by with a rack of books.
losing, sir. You can't stay here. We're shut-

ng all at sea. "I lost track of the time,

s up here. I was talking to him
y. I saw you several times,
nowhere. I figured you

adows and the

voman
ps a

a couple of fellows sat and talked with me of the day and t

weather and the sports—nothing of consequence.

Just once, I thought I saw Garnet, sitting in the shadows

laughing at my confusion, but when I looked again, ther

nothing but shadow and a mystery.

LAST WORI

I'd been storytelling for h

caught in some kind of

up, and except for me

the upstairs of the

empty.

I cleared my th

spell," I said.

Garnet nodded

ghost of a smile.

"Now that's a fine string

he said. "Fancy and imagination, a wink

and a grin. A hint of magic and the mer-

est bone of fact. Yes sir, you are a story-

teller, and I take my hat off to you."

He tipped his hat and bowed, and

then the lights dimmed in the Archives.

There was a soft flicker like a bit of heat

lightning, and I felt a chill run barefoot

across my soul.